Cider

in Sidmouth

Cidered in Sidmouth

AN EAST DEVON COSY MYSTERY

P.A. NASH

This is a work of fiction.

Similarities to real people, places, or events are entirely coincidental.

Cidered in Sidmouth

Copyright © 2019 PA Nash.

Written by PA Nash.

All rights reserved. This book or any portion thereof may not be reproduced or used in any manner whatsoever without the express written permission of the publisher except for the use of brief quotations in a book review.

First Published 2019

This edition 2021

www.eastdevoncosymysteries.com

Cover picture by P.A. Nash

DEDICATION

To the whole Nash family –
from Elsie's Bow to Resource Angel,
not forgetting the family genealogist.
Love from PA.

ACKNOWLEDGMENTS

"Many of the places mentioned in this book do exist. Some of the places exist only in the figment of my imagination. I'll leave it up to you to come to Sidmouth and the rest of East Devon to find out which are which."

"This is Sidmouth, sir. Nobody gets murdered in Sidmouth!"

Newly retired Frank and Ella Raleigh didn't expect to be confronted with an upturned body in a cider barrel. WPC Knowle called it a tragic accident, Frank and Ella didn't agree. Guess who was right?

Welcome to East Devon, land of cider, scenery and cream teas.

If you enjoy pacy whodunit cosy mysteries set in our glorious East Devon countryside, then join Frank and Ella in the Regency seaside resort of Sidmouth, as they seek to find who murdered Billy Bowd.

Cidered in Sidmouth brings you coastal walks, cider farms, cliff-top drama and a traditional Golden Age denouement as Frank and Ella solve the clues to a very unusual murder in this quiet old-fashioned seaside town.

A gentle cosy read in the tradition of Midsomer and the two Agathas.

Treasure the walks. Uncover the clues. Solve the mystery.

PA Nash has written a cosy mystery blending murder with scenic local walks and landmarks.

"A very easy read ideal for holiday reading. "

"A pleasant and easy read enhanced the lovely description of Sidmouth and the local walks. Good introduction to the characters who run through the series."

TABLE OF CONTENTS

Chapter One	1
Chapter Two	2
Chapter Three	9
Chapter Four	18
Chapter Five	23
Chapter Six	29
Chapter Seven	38
Chapter Eight	43
Chapter Nine	52
Chapter Ten	67
Chapter Eleven	79
Chapter Twelve	84
Chapter Thirteen	93
Chapter Fourteen	102
Chapter Fifteen	109
Chapter Sixteen	119
Chapter Seventeen	124
Chapter Eighteen	131
Chapter Nineteen	139
Chapter Twenty	143
Postscript	145
A good walk	146
About the Author	149
Also Available	150
Excerpt from The Dudleys of Budleigh	153

CHAPTER ONE

YOU'VE RUINED EVERYTHING

You've ruined everything. How dare you think you can get away with it.

The vase was within reach. Picking it up in anger with no thought for the consequences, it was a simple and automatic action to crash it down on his head. The man stumbled backwards, ricocheted off the single armchair in the room and fell headfirst on the stone floor.

There was silence. Not even a moan.

I've killed him.

CHAPTER TWO

A MIS-DELIVERED PACKAGE

The postman took three hours to deliver a giant roll of bubble wrap. Someone told him, "Pop it in the corner."

Retirement is wonderful, Frank thought. No more pressure and stress. No more looking at the clock. No more living by other people's expectations. No more... well, everything.

Now, there's time to while away. Old friends to greet, new friends to meet. Time to enjoy the pleasure of enjoying time well spent. Like today. The autumn sun was lighting up the top of the trees, there was a breeze to just keep it this side of cool, the leaves were floating sporadically to the moist earth and Frank and Ella were strolling with another couple, Bella and George, friends from the village. They were heading through the woods along the old railway track from the Bowd down towards Harpford.

"Couldn't have done this ten years ago."

"No, we would've been too busy mollycoddling teachers," Ella smiled, "and then endlessly trying to see the best in children."

"Yes, rather than seeing the best of each other and this glorious countryside."

Frank never regretted for one nanosecond taking early retirement and moving down here to East Devon. Particularly on a carefree day like today.

"Autumn is definitely one of the best four seasons." Bella sighed.

They crossed over the East Devon Way footpath and followed the old railway track down to Knapp's Lane. Here they branched off to the right and ambled back over the stone bridge and into the pretty village of Harpford. They walked past the medieval church of St Gregory the Great. Crossing the River Otter by the rickety metal bridge, they trudged through the muddy field that led back to the Recreation Ground car-park. Here they bid each other farewell and both couples headed for their village homes.

Ella had enjoyed the walk and the companionship of their two friends. Retirement is wonderful. Except... you need a routine. You need something to live for. A reason to get up in the morning. You need interests and enthusiasms. At the moment, Ella wasn't totally sold on retirement.

At home, hidden somewhat obviously besides the green garden waste bin, was a small brown paper package that wouldn't fit through their letterbox. Ella picked it up before heading indoors. They made their usual cups of coffee and tea before Ella went to open the package. She wasn't expecting a delivery because she had bought nothing online in the last week. Ella stopped and examined the writing on the front.

"They've done it again. Almost the right address, totally the wrong location."

Living in River Street, Otterbury caused no end of problems to the jolly postmen at the local sorting office. They were forever getting mail intended for River Street in Sidmouth. Most of the time, Ella just underlined the postcode and put it back in the post-box down by the war memorial.

This time the autumnal sunshine was promising to continue and Sidmouth was a wonderful place in which to wander around. Being out of season, you could park the car without too many problems.

"Why don't we find out where this doppelganger lives?"

Frank put down the local paper. "What are you talking about?"

"This package. It's not for us. It should be for River Street in Sidmouth."

"Not again. Surely someone must be able to read in the Post Office. This never used to happen when we were in Kent. Well, not as often."

"They sort it by machine these days, Frank!"

"Well, they ought to sort it out. Can I see how they messed it up this time?"

Frank took the package before bursting into laughter.

"They haven't even got the number correct. Look, it says 23. Since when have we lived at 23? The sorting machine can't read. 23 is an age I'd love to be once again, but it's nowhere near our address."

"If you were 23, then we wouldn't have been married all these years!"

"Right, scrub my last comment. Where was it posted?"

"Postmarked Cullompton."

"Local post office sorters should know better. Surely they know this is not Sidmouth?"

"I suppose the sorting machine could have mistaken the postcode for ours."

"It's written so scruffily. Someone was in a hurry." Frank put the package back down on the table.

"I'm going to phone the sorting office in Sidmouth about this. It happens all too often."

The automated phone message told them that this call may be recorded for monitoring and training purposes. Then Frank was connected to a gentleman who took their name and address, the details of the package and apologised for the mis-delivery. He suggested taking the package to the nearest post office and asking them to post it to the correct address. Then before Frank could vent any amount of scorn upon the Post Office, the line went dead. Frank stared at the phone before putting it down on its stand.

Ella watched his face become even more thunderous.

"Frank, you need to calm down. It's most unlike you. Let's have dinner and then we'll go into Sidmouth this afternoon, deliver the package to the correct address, have a walk along the seafront and grab an ice cream at Taste."

Taste was one of Sidmouth's secret delights. The best ice cream outside of Cornwall with a multitude of flavours and always exceedingly generous portions.

Frank visibly relaxed. "Good plan. Who'd have thought we'd be eating ice cream at the seaside in October."

Sidmouth had a reputation in some circles as the regency preserve of the elderly and infirm. Today that appeared to be so true as evidenced by the ponderous speed of much of the traffic. The ten-minute journey took well over double the usual time. The sunny weather was more like June than October. It had brought tourists and elderly locals out onto the streets. In the High Street, two large cars were attempting to reverse into spaces in which only a motorbike could safely park. The result was gridlock. Frank eventually was able to turn off left and sidle into the car park that only the locals know. He was grateful to find a space. They paid for an hour at the ticket machine and were soon nimbly dodging the dawdling crowds in their quest to find 23, River Street.

"It's so busy today." Ella had to shout as a muddy quad bike with an even muddier trailer zoomed up the narrow road past them. Ella stared at it as it roared around the corner.

There were houses with numbers and no names, houses with names but no numbers and a couple with neither names nor numbers. They were interspersed with a couple of shops that had names but never any numbers.

A group of cyclists travelling three abreast passed them by. The group included two couples on bright red and orange tandems. Ella smiled at them and called out "Lovely afternoon!"

They all looked at her with disdain and carried on holding up a queue of cars behind them. Ella raised her eyebrows. "All sorts out today!"

Eventually, they found what appeared to be the right address. It was the end house of a terrace-a small trio of mellow red brick Edwardian dwellings. Frank called them two up, two downs. Ella called them quaint. Next door, separated by a walled alleyway, was The Mariner pub.

"I didn't know this pub was here. I've never heard of it before."

"Doesn't look too grand. Could be one to explore in the future." Frank added as he opened the black rusting metal gate that led up a short, uneven flagstone path.

The blue painted door was flanked by two flowerpots. Both had the remains of last year's annuals. Ella could not find a bell, so she knocked gently on the door. No-one answered.

"Can't we just leave the package on the doorstep and go for our ice-cream?" she said.

"Knock again-but louder."

Ella did so with the same result.

"If this were Otterbury, then someone would have left the key underneath the flowerpot," Frank chuckled.

"But it's not... This is Sidmouth."

"No harm in checking." Frank knelt and lifted up the right-hand flowerpot and looked underneath.

"I don't believe it!" whispered Ella.

Frank picked up a sturdy looking latchkey and tried it in the lock. The key turned, the door opened, and Frank stuck his head inside before calling out. "Hello, anybody home? We've got a package for you!"

No-one answered.

"Hello?" repeated Frank.

"Just leave it on the doormat!" Ella was pleased that no-one was home. It would avoid a discussion about the Post Office, or even worse, the incorrect addressing of too much post these days. They would now just deposit the package and head off towards the seafront.

Frank had other ideas. Taking the package from Ella, he disappeared into, what he assumed to be, a hallway. He put it down on a small circular table hidden behind the front door.

"Wait a minute. I'm going to leave a note with the package. Have you got a pen and paper?"

Ella shook her head.

"Well, in that case, I'm just going to find something to write on in one of the rooms. I'll be straight back."

He called out again, "Hello, anybody in?"

There was no reply. As he ventured further into the house, Ella called out to him, "I'm not staying out here in full view of the suspicious Sidmouth public. I'm coming in as well!"

Frank casually walked into the front room. Ella looked around to see if anyone nearby was watching them and then quickly followed.

The room was dark, sparsely furnished and unkempt. A stone floor, a single battered old sea-blue armchair and a couple of stacked wooden chairs. No television, the remains of a coal fire in a dirty grate. The curtains were half-open, but the windows were opaque with smudges of dirt. On the mantelpiece was a photo of a man and a woman, smiling lovingly at each other.

Getting accustomed to the lack of light, they could both see that someone had been having a severe disagreement. A coffee table lay overturned with its magazines and newspapers scattered on a threadbare rug. Two cushions from the armchair were also on the stone floor by the fireplace. Ella bent to pick one up and immediately jumped back with a startled "Oh! Frank, come here. Is this blood on the floor? Here, by the fireplace."

Frank had just opened the door leading to a back room which appeared to be a kitchen. Before he went in, he turned back towards Ella to examine the patch. Picking the other cushion off the floor, he let out a similar cry.

"You're right. It certainly looks like blood. Put the cushions back, exactly where you found them. Let's check out the rest of the house."

Ella hastily replaced the cushions and stepped around the scattered papers and magazines before following Frank into the kitchen. From here, they could see a sight that would take them a very long time to forget.

"Ella, have you got your phone with you?"

The back door was open and, in full view, on the right-hand side of the tiny paved and gravelled courtyard stood a huge wooden Cider Vat. It was quite the largest barrel that either had ever seen. Sticking out from the top of the vat were two bare legs.

CHAPTER THREE

IS THAT BILLY'S LEGS?

I want to die like my grandfather, peacefully in his sleep. Not screaming and terrified, like the passengers on his bus.

"Frank, is that a person?" Ella's voice was on the verge of cracking. "What? What are they doing upside down in the Cider Vat?"

"Ella, just phone the police. There's no movement. I'm pretty sure whoever is in there is dead!"

Ella's face expressed her shock. Without another word, she turned slowly back into the kitchen, took out her mobile from the pocket of her jeans and dialled 999. Frank took ten seconds worth of deep breaths. After a protracted silence, Ella started to report the incident.

Frank, feeling slightly more in control of himself, began to look around the courtyard. The Cider Vat must have been full of liquid because there were wet spillages all over the courtyard's paving stones and gravel. It smelt like cider. Frank knew the barrel was a cider vat due to the lettering wrapped around the middle of the vat – Sowden Valley Farm Cider.

The bare hairy legs looked like a man's. It didn't take much brain to guess that this might well be the homeowner.

The barrel was huge. It looked like a Tun Barrel. He'd only been reading about Devonshire Cider farms the other day in a local magazine. The Tun Barrel was the biggest – over two hundred gallons.

But why on earth would anyone want to climb head-first into such a barrel? And then get stuck and be unable to get out again? Especially when it's full of cider. No-one gets that thirsty! Could it have been a horrible accident? If so, what a way to go!

He went back into the kitchen searching for the name of the owner of the house. On the wall, a cork noticeboard, next to the only kitchen cupboard, was covered with paper bills and official letters. It didn't take long for Frank to deduce the homeowner was one Billy Bowd. Was he the dead man?

He went back out to the courtyard. On the gravel were scuff marks. Some of them were mixed with blood. Yes, there were drops of blood on the paving stones as well. Did he do that? Did he tread in any of the spots of blood in the front room? He couldn't really remember. All he could remember was coming out of the kitchen and seeing the barrel and the bare legs.

Both Frank and Ella had read enough detective books to know that they must touch nothing else. It was called Contaminating the Evidence.

Ella had finished on her mobile and came back out into the courtyard. She stood beside Frank, staring at the barrel. Frank put his arm around her shoulders but said nothing.

"They're sending a constable. He'll be here as soon as possible." Ella's voice was stronger, but she was unable to conceal her shock.

"We'd better go indoors and wait."

They turned to go back into the kitchen. Ella sat down at the table.

"I'm going to take a quick look around."

"Don't go!" Ella stood up, deliberately facing away from the courtyard.

"I'll be one minute at most. Shout if you need me!"

Frank left the room. Ella awkwardly sat back down. She stared at the cork noticeboard not daring to turn around and look out into the courtyard.

She could hear Frank clomping around upstairs. A minute can be a very long time. She hoped he wouldn't be much longer.

A piercing scream hit her full in the face.

"Billy, what you done with Billy?"

A woman with long purple straggly hair, wearing a vivid flowery purple summer dress and clad in red Doc Marten boots, stood in the middle of the kitchen. She waved her arms and breathed as if she was about to give birth.

"Good afternoon, young lady. And who might you be?" Ella quietly replied, disguising a feeling of growing fear.

"Don't you give me all that posh talk rubbish, old woman. I want to know what you done with Billy? How did you get in here? The front door was wide open."

Frank had heard the commotion and rapidly re-appeared in the kitchen. He stepped in between the two women. "I think my wife asked who you might be. Why don't we all sit down here at the kitchen table and converse like three intelligent, civilised human beings?"

Amazingly enough, purple straggly hair complied with the polite request. Frank made sure he sat in the middle of the three.

"Right, my name is Frank. This is my wife Ella. And you are…?"

"Amelia - Amelia Nutwell. I'm Billy's girlfriend. So missie, don't try any la-di-da moves on my Billy."

Somehow Ella couldn't prevent a watery smile.

"And you can wipe that smile off your pretty face!"

Frank diverted purple straggly hair's attention back to him. "We are here because we were delivering a package that had been misdirected to us at our house. The key was under the flowerpot by the front door."

"Well, I know that. I've got my own key, so I don't need the spare."

"Now, Amelia," Frank continued, "we may have some bad news for you."

Ella thought that Amelia seemed to sense what Frank was about to tell her.

"We think that your Billy may be out in the courtyard in the cider vat barrel."

Amelia laughed and got up so she could see out of the closed kitchen door into the courtyard.

"There's somebody in the barrel! He's upside down. Is that Billy's legs?"

"Has he got a tattoo on either leg?"

"Yes, on his calf. It's meant to be like that barrel. He's only just had it done."

Frank had noticed the strange tattoo. It appeared to be a cider vat. It was way too similar to the barrel in the courtyard.

"Then it could be Billy?"

"I can see a tattoo. My word, I can see a tattoo!"

Ella tried soothingly to join in with the conversation. "We've called the police. They should be here any minute now."

Amelia turned away from the door. "The police? I'm not speaking to any police. No. Not the police. You can deal with it. You killed him; you face the consequences. They'll put you in jail!"

Amelia headed for the open back door, and almost ran into the courtyard. The ridiculous accusation left Frank and Ella stunned. They did nothing to stop her.

Ella was only able to shout, "Don't touch anything!"

Amelia had no intention. They heard a terrifying scream and then nothing. Within a couple of seconds, she had disappeared.

"Wait a minute, you can't just run away! The police will want to speak to you if you're his girlfriend…" Frank was speaking into thin air. He got up and followed her into the courtyard.

Frank shouted out to Ella, "She's not here!"

"How did she get out of the courtyard. Over the wall?"

"No, they're too tall to climb over. There must be a door or a gate here somewhere."

Frank looked around, avoiding the barrel and its pair of legs. The courtyard was rectangular with two brick walls and a tall wooden fence reaching easily six foot in height. The back of the house made up the fourth side of the rectangle. Frank reckoned the courtyard was no bigger than four metres in depth. There was no gate. The brick walls were solid and as tall as the fence. Frank was increasingly baffled until he made himself look at the barrel. He immediately understood how Amelia had disappeared.

However, he had no time to consider any pursuit. There was a sharp knock on the front door and in strode a young, efficient looking policewoman.

"Hello, we received a call about a dead body. I'm WPC Knowle and this is PC Hydon. At least, it will be if he can find his way into the house." She turned around to look behind her, waited for a moment and then returned his gaze upon the couple.

"And you are, sir, and madam?"

"My name is Frank, and this is Ella, my wife. Frank and Ella Raleigh."

WPC Knowle jotted the names down in her black notebook. A

loud thump on the door announced the arrival of PC Hydon. Neither Frank nor Ella had ever seen such an enormous human being, let alone a police officer. He filled his uniform both length-ways and width-ways. He must have had to remove his hat and duck his head to get through the door and into the room.

"Right, now we're both here, perhaps you can tell us why we've been summoned?"

Frank moved away from the door into the courtyard and faced the two police officers.

"We had a package wrongly delivered to our address. It's not the first time so we decided to deliver it personally. We knocked on the front door here but no-one answered. We couldn't post the package through the letterbox. I found a key under the flowerpot and tried it in the front door. It turned the latch, so we came in. I was going to leave the package on the kitchen table with a note but when we got to the kitchen, we looked out into the courtyard and saw that."

He pointed to the cider barrel.

"My word, what's his legs be doing upside-down like that?" blustered PC Hydon, "He be drowning if 'e's not careful."

"I think he's beyond that," said Ella.

Both police officers strolled out in the courtyard and surveyed the scene.

"How sad, how very sad." WPC Knowle touched the ankle of the deceased, "Definitely dead. What a tragic accident. He must have stood on the step there and slipped in."

"Yes, 'e got stuck and couldn't get out again. What a way to go."

"This is cider, isn't it?" WPC Knowle dipped a finger into the liquid.

"So, he drank himself to death?"

"What a way to go!" PC Hydon repeated.

Both Frank and Ella stared at each other.

"Don't you think it could be foul play? He may have been murdered!"

PC Hydon turned around and spoke incredulously:

"This is Sidmouth, sir. Nobody gets murdered in Sidmouth!"

Other official people arrived and extracted the body from the barrel and took him away. Frank had seen a photo of Billy Bowd in the front room. The corpse's face was already bloated and reddened but was definitely Billy. Even the police agreed with that. PC Hydon slumped himself down into the large tatty armchair in the front room and began to take notes.

Frank and Ella were asked to make themselves available to pop into the Police Station so they could make a statement. Another person busied themselves in securing both front and back doors. It appeared that was that.

"Wait a minute, please," cried Ella. "Aren't you missing out on some very significant clues?"

Frank agreed, "Yes, the front room is a wreck. It looks like a fight took place in there. There are blood stains by the fire. Somebody tried to cover them up with cushions. It all appears to be very suspicious and upstairs…"

Frank paused for breath.

"Yes, I had noticed the state of the front room," replied WPC Knowle. "But, sir, there could be any number of reasons for the mess. Did he live alone?"

"There's a picture of a happy couple on the mantelpiece," Ella pointed.

PC Hydon perked up. "When they took him out, I noticed a wedding ring on his finger."

"So, we may need to contact a Mrs. Bowd." WPC Knowle took

more notes.

"What about the blood on the floor?"

"He may have cut himself and couldn't bear to see it. Lots of people can't stand the sight of blood."

Ella suddenly remembered the purple straggly haired lady.

"But while we were waiting for you, we had a visitor. A wild woman, name of Amelia Nutwell. She claimed to be Billy's girlfriend."

"Where is she now?"

"We told her we were waiting for the police and then she scampered out through the kitchen door into the courtyard."

"That's strange." WPC Knowle struck a thoughtful pose. "I didn't see a back gate in the courtyard."

There was a brief moment of silence whilst the woman police officer scribbled away.

"Right, we must be getting on. We have to cover a large area of East Devon and I bet, there's a list a mile long waiting for me in the police car. If you'd like to leave through the front door, I'll close everything up behind me."

PC Hydon got up from the armchair. "Cheers," he said as he walked out of the front door.

WPC Knowle frowned at her partner and then turned to smile at Frank and Ella.

"I'll see you tomorrow at the police station? For your statement? Do you know where we are? Turn up at eleven and ask for WPC Knowle. We'll sort it all out then!" She stood there, ushering the couple on their way.

Frank and Ella left the building in a trance and walked, hand in hand, back to the car park. All thoughts of ice cream had vanished from their minds a long time ago. All they wanted to do now was to go home.

They arrived back at the car-park to find, attached firmly to the windscreen of their car, a parking ticket.

CHAPTER FOUR

CIDERED IN SIDMOUTH

Knowledge is knowing a tomato is a fruit; Wisdom is not putting it in a fruit salad.

"We help report a suspicious death," Frank blustered, "and we get a parking ticket as a reward!"

He was fuming as he snatched from the windscreen the plastic envelope containing the ticket.

Ella didn't know whether to laugh or cry.

"Don't worry. We'll dispute it tomorrow when we make our statement. Let's just go home."

They drove slowly from the car-park, through the narrow back-streets of old Sidmouth, turned right to head along the seafront.

The tourists were still out and about and the regency sea-front was covered with couples strolling and seagulls swooping. Elderly ladies and gentlemen were perched on wooden council benches chatting and people watching. Here and there, younger couples, some with toddlers, some with babies in prams, stared wistfully at the pebbles between them and the sea. Did they realise that if they had only gone to Exmouth they could have spent the whole day on a sandy beach?

Ella turned inland up Station Road past the Knowle towards the old railway station.

Soon, Frank and Ella were comfortably seated in their own front room overlooking the hills dividing the Otter and the Sid valleys. Confronted by the patchwork of fields, populated by grazing sheep and cows, Sidmouth now seemed to be on another planet.

Both sat there in peace and solitude for some minutes, going over the afternoon's calamitous events. Neither of them had experienced anything quite like the last couple of hours.

Ella broke the silence.

"What did you mean about upstairs? What did you see?"

"A couple of strange things. In the bedroom, there were clothes all over the floor."

"I'm not surprised given the state of the front room."

"Yes, but the clothes were in pieces. It looked like someone had taken a pair of large scissors to them."

"Were they his clothes?"

"I think so. But there were so many bits…"

Ella frowned. "And the other strange thing?"

"There was a phone by the bed."

"Don't tell me, someone had ripped it from the wall!"

"No. It was one of those with an answer-phone attached. I just had time to listen to the messages. There were only two of them. The first was from someone called Gabriel saying he needed to speak to him about some more gallons."

"Cider?" was Ella's educated guess.

"Could be. The other was from a woman demanding he pays her what was rightfully hers. If not, he was in big trouble."

"I bet that was the ex-wife." Ella was on a roll. "Now that could explain the cut-up clothing!"

"Do you think purple straggly hair was his wife? She said her name was Amelia Nutwell. Could be her maiden name?"

"Could be, but she didn't look anything like the woman in the photo."

They sat there, once again, in silence. They were both taking in all the information and its suspicious connotations. As teachers, they had been used to sorting out problems between children. Sifting the evidence and drawing mostly accurate conclusions. This was undoubtedly different.

"Anything else?"

"No, not upstairs. But on the mantle-piece was a postcard."

"Yes, I saw you slip that into your back pocket when the police weren't looking."

"Oh, I thought I got away with that!"

Frank took the postcard out of his pocket. "There was a picture on the front of some apples. They were speckled red and green, varied in size and shape."

"Well, is it important?"

"I don't know, I haven't time to read it yet."

"Look, there's no address. Just these words." Frank showed the writing to Ella. She read it out loud.

"Billy Bowd Pippin! The recipe's worth a lot to us and to you. We'll be in touch!"

"And it's signed…"

"The Zummerzet Zyder Mafia!"

"Who on earth are the Zummerzet Zyder Mafia?"

"Well, they must be from Somerset. They have a vested interest in Cider, and they sound as if they're criminals."

"A very obvious deduction!" Ella laughed.

"Very strange." Frank rubbed his chin, "This tragic accident is looking more and more suspicious."

"Do you really think, it could be murder?"

"The caption of the photo reads Billy Down Pippin. That's the name of the apples." Ella turned the postcard back over to look at the picture.

"Billy Down Pippin? Billy Bowd Pippin? They knew his name. It's a warning aimed at him!"

Ella mused for a moment. "Poor Billy Bowd - Cidered in Sidmouth!"

Once again, they sat in silence engrossed in their own thoughts as they sipped their cups of tea.

"Wait a minute," Ella said, "Could anyone, a random person, just have broken in? Maybe a burglar?"

"There were no signs of damage to either the front or back door. The back door was open. They could have escaped that way. The front door only opened when we used the key. The key was still there under the flowerpot."

"In that case, if it was murder, he must have opened one of the doors to let his killer into the house!"

They both lapsed back into companionable silence. Being married for nearly forty years they knew exactly what the other was contemplating.

Frank put their thoughts into words. "It must be either a ghastly accident or… wilful murder!"

Ella nodded. "And I think it's more than likely to be wilful murder. There's at least four suspects from our knowledge alone!

"The ex-wife, Amelia 'purple straggly haired' Nutwell, Gabriel from the answer-phone and the Zummerzet Mafia."

"It could be any one of them!"

"'Ello, be that the Sidmouth Herald? Good. I've got 'ee a stary. A stary fer your nooospaper. There be a man stuck in 'is cider vat. 'Is legs upalong pointing to the sky. He's as apple pied as a cider drinker affer harvest. Dead drunk. No, oi'm a nony mouse, a concerned reader. Cheers."

"Aretha, there's some bloke on the phone. Talking about a body in a cider vat. Says he was dead drunk."

"Yeah, he sounds it! Look, put the phone down. There's no story in a drunkard's ramblings. We've got more important things to cover. There's a town council committee meeting. They're discussing moving one of the council noticeboards and painting it red."

CHAPTER FIVE

THERE'S NO SUCH THING AS UNFORTUNATE COINCIDENCES

The search for someone to blame is always successful.

Frank and Ella attended the police station the following day, keen to share their thoughts and eyewitness evidence.

WPC Knowle took them to a side room, offered them a cup of tea and sat them down on two black rickety plastic chairs in front of an old Formica-topped table.

"Welcome, Mr. and Mrs. Raleigh. Just tell me, step by step, what happened. From the time you arrived at the house on River Street to the time you left. Just to let you know, I'm recording this. Then, I can concentrate on your story without having to worry about writing it all down for now. I will type it up later and ask you to sign the statement once you've agreed it's a true record!"

Frank and Ella went through the events together. The misdelivered package, the key under the flowerpot, the messy front room and the discovery of the body.

Once or twice, they had to correct or clarify something with each other. Occasionally, WPC Knowle interrupted to ask a question.

Frank recounted his quick look-around upstairs. Ella told of her abrupt meeting with Amelia Nutwell and her rapid appearance and then disappearance. They both described the contents of the cider barrel. Frank even confessed to the borrowing of the postcard. He handed it back to the smiling policewoman and apologised for his foolish behaviour.

Whenever either Frank or Ella voiced an opinion, WPC Knowle gently reminded them to keep to the facts and not to drift into the realms of speculation.

It took a while but, eventually, they were both satisfied that they had remembered everything. The recorder was turned off and WPC Knowle thanked them for their thoroughness and clarity.

"It makes a change to hear two people give their evidence in such a clear manner."

"Thank you," said Ella, "but what happens next?"

"I think I mentioned about typing it all up and…"

"Yes, with respect, I know about that. What I meant is what are you going to do about Billy Bowd's death?"

"Well, my Sergeant will pass on all the evidence we've gathered to his superiors. Somebody somewhere will decide if an inquest is needed. The coroner will be informed and, after all that, I expect someone will declare the death to be a tragic accident with no further action to be taken."

"But, it seemed to us, that there was every chance that it could have been murder." Frank kept his voice calm and steady.

Ella copied his persona. "Or manslaughter, at the very least!"

"That's one way of looking at it, but it seems to me more likely to be a tragic accident. Your clues can be interpreted as unfortunate coincidences. No, I think accidental death will be the verdict."

Frank and Ella stared first at WPC Knowle and then at each

other.

"I'm sorry, I don't agree with you. There's no such thing as unfortunate coincidences."

"Can we have a look around the house again, please?" asked Ella.

"I don't think that would be a good idea. Besides, I expect the house to be included in the will and the ex-wife soon to be its new owner. Unless, of course, Billy Bowd changed the will in favour of his girlfriend, Amelia."

"Is there nothing we can do to make you change your mind?"

"Not unless you two Sherlocks bring me some evidence! No, seriously, that was just my little joke. Don't get involved. It isn't worth your time. You've done an excellent job in allowing us to have a clear picture of the gruesome events. But now, for you, it's over. You must have plenty of other activities to fill up your life."

All three of them suffered a short, almost embarrassed silence.

"Well, thank you for coming. I'll let you know when it's all typed up and when you need to come back in to sign the statement. I'll show you out now and bid you good morning."

And that was that.

Frank and Ella decided to head for Taste and buy the ice-cream that they intended to enjoy the day before. Large Black Cherry cone for Frank. Honeycomb and Ginger for Ella. The best value ice creams in town were consumed and fully appreciated as they sat in Market Square, the pedestrianised area between Taste and the promenade. Seagulls were infamous in Sidmouth for swooping down on unsuspecting tourists who chose to lick their ice-cream cones on the promenade. The gulls attacked like low flying aircraft before escaping with their cold and creamy reward. Wily locals, therefore, tended to finish their cones in and around Market Square before venturing onto the prom.

When they had regretfully finished, they ventured past a clutch of gift shops and cafes and navigated the pedestrian crossing onto the promenade. The quiet retiring couples and childless family groups walking by provided Frank and Ella with some gentle minutes of entertainment. Although out of season, Sidmouth had learned, particularly in recent years, to cater to the empty-nesters and gentle folk who enjoyed the ambience of a Regency style seaside town. This less fashionable haven prided itself in being devoid of the commercialised attractions of some less cultured resorts further down the Devon coast.

Occasionally, walkers equipped with a rucksack and solid walking boots, passed them by as they strode along one of the few urban sections of the South West Coast Path. Normally, in East Devon, the six hundred and thirty-three mile long path was known for its succession of climbs up to cliff-top views followed by descents into river valleys. Here in Sidmouth, the coast path became one mile of flat, straight tarmac.

The sky was painted Devonian Blue and sprinkled with pure white fluffy clouds. The sea was calm and almost Mediterranean in its colour. Frank and Ella lounged contentedly against the promenade railings for half an hour. Moments like this reminded them why they had moved down to the West Country.

Eventually, Ella murmured, "Time to go home." They headed slowly back to their car, Frank's arm loosely around Ella's shoulder. Passing the Anchor Inn in Old Fore Street, they heard, before they saw, two women discussing the empty state of their forlorn world.

"He owed me money. He hadn't paid me for 4 months."

"You're bloomin' lucky. I was supporting him, despite the

fact, that he was working up at Sowden Valley."

A slow slurp of cider filled the abbreviated gap.

"And now Billy Down Pippin's gone and left us like a lifeboat with no crew! What are we going to do?"

As they drew alongside, Ella stopped and smiled.

"Excuse me, I couldn't help hearing, but were you talking about Billy Bowd?"

One of the women looked up at her from her tankard.

"Oh, it's you again!"

Ella immediately recognised her as Amelia Nutwell - the lady in purple.

Amelia pointed menacingly at Ella, "'Ere, Agnes, it's that 'orrible woman and her partner. Again."

"Not the one who you said was after him in the Byes that time?"

"No, no, no. That one was much younger… and far prettier!"

Ella blushed with indignation.

"No, this one," continued Amelia, "was at the house when I found Billy's body. I think she had something to do with his death. I can't prove it and I ain't gonna yap to the police but…"

Frank intervened. "Excuse me, ladies. We had nothing to do with Billy's death. We never even knew the man. We were returning a misdirected postal delivery."

"La-di-da language! Misdirected postal delivery! Haa!" She turned her bitter words once more towards Ella. "Perhaps you were having an affair with him behind my back. Does he know?" Amelia tilted her head towards Frank.

At last, Ella found her voice- "Don't be preposterous. I love my husband and he loves me. We've been very happy together for over 30 years!"

"Maybe, but you seem to be popping up all over the place.

Are you following me around?"

Frank laughed. "Sidmouth is a small place, and this is only the second time we've clapped eyes on you. The first time you left rather promptly."

Ella's voice went up in pitch and volume. "In fact, you should know the police found your disappearance very strange. They're probably looking for you. You'd better get your story sorted out before they catch up with you."

Frank intervened again, "That's enough, Ella. I'm sure Amelia and Agnes will be contacting the police to explain everything."

"Yeah, shut up and go away," growled Amelia. "We've both had quite a shock. Let two old friends drink in peace."

Agnes turned to Amelia, ignoring Frank and Ella," We could go back to Billy's house like we normally do. I've still got a key to get in with. Forgot to give it back to Billy!"

"Oh yeah, I believe you. No, I ain't going back there again. Probably cursed or something."

Ella tried one last time. "How long have you two been old friends? A bit strange to see the ex-wife and girlfriend together."

"Be off with you. Mind your own business, if you know what's good for you," said Amelia.

"Yeah, scram," said Agnes, looking at Ella for the first time, "If I find out you've been seeing my old man, my ex-old man, for business purposes or any other reason, then I'm going find a cider vat big enough to fit you in. Clear off!"

CHAPTER SIX

FOUR SUSPECTS

Better to remain silent and be thought a fool, than to speak and remove all doubt.

Billy Bowd's funeral took place at All Saints' Church two weeks later. The attendance was sparse. Frank and Ella thought it too obvious to attend. However, they just happened to be sitting in the Mustard Seed café, across from the church. They were drinking coffee and enjoying a generous slice of walnut cake before, during and after the short service.

They both took careful note of the attendees. Amelia and Agnes came in together, both dressed modestly in black. WPC Knowle walked into the church car park, out of uniform but distinctly police-like in her manner. Two men came in separately. They neither looked at or talked to each other, but Ella got the impression that they may have been acquaintances of some kind.

"Work colleagues from Sowden Valley?"

"Sowden Valley?" Frank looked blank.

"Yes, that was the lettering on the Cider Vat."

"Of course, but where is Sowden Valley?" Frank took out his phone and googled the words.

"Sowden Valley Cider Farm is up near Clyst St Lawrence."

"Where's that?" asked Ella.

"Cullompton way."

"We need to check that out." Ella's gaze was drawn to some further arrivals. "Frank, look over there. Is that not the Frost Report sketch come to life?"

"The one with John Cleese, Ronnie Barker and Ronnie Corbett?"

"Yes, I know my place!"

Three black-suited gentlemen of distinctly different heights, all wearing sunglasses, stood at the entrance to the church car park. They loitered for a few minutes and then decided against going in. Instead, they made their way across the road and entered the Mustard Seed café. They sat down at a window table with a good view of the church entrance. They removed their sunglasses and stared intently out of the window.

"They're doing exactly what we're doing!" whispered Ella.

"Yes. Spying!"

The tallest of them ordered a pot of tea and some biscuits.

Frank and Ella couldn't avoid hearing their conversation, however quiet they intended it to be.

"Dreadful turn out," the tall one remarked.

"Yes, but it'll still be ages yet. It's Devon time remember."

"As slow as a rush-hour tractor."

"We'll need to speak to Gabriel."

"We could have gone in."

"No, there were so few people we'd have stuck out like an apple in a vineyard," said the short one. He continued. "Like a spider in a soup bowl."

There was a moment of silence then once again he muttered, "Like a baby in a manger!"

"What are you talking about? Be quiet if you can't say

anything constructive."

"Steer clear of 'arry," the short one mumbled.

"Now, just shut up and keep your eyes focused over there."

Frank and Ella mentally added two new names to their list.

Ten minutes later the three gentlemen resumed their conversation.

"Death jokes. We need cheering up." Yet again the short one interrupted the silence. The other two ignored him.

"Alright, I'll start. How does a Devonian drown a fish? Don't know? He puts it in water! Geddit?"

There was still no reaction from the other two. Other customers in the Mustard Seed looked at him with some bewilderment.

"I got another. How do you drown a Devonian? Not a fish this time. Don't you know? You put a scratch and sniff card at the bottom of a bathtub!"

"What if it's got no water in it?" asked the tall one.

A member of staff behind the counter shook her head in sympathy.

"Alright, one more and then it's your turn. About a month before he died, my uncle had his back covered in lard. You don't know why, do you? Well, after that, he went downhill fast."

"Did he really?" remarked the short one.

"No, it's a joke!"

"Really? A joke? I suggest you finish up your tea and wipe the biscuit crumbs from around your mouth with your serviette."

The member of staff behind the counter nodded her head this time.

Ella whispered, "Frank, I've got one. If you run in front of a car you'll get tired, but if you run behind the car you'll get exhausted."

Frank smiled, finished his tea and poured them both another cup.

Twenty minutes later there was a stirring of action from across the road.

The short one again spoke quietly but loud enough for Frank and Ella to hear. "Watch out, action stations! Finish up."

The coffin was placed with dignity into the hearse. The ushers removed their hats and climbed into the vehicle which turned right, out of the church car park, before driving slowly in the direction of Exeter.

The tall one turned to the others. "Right, let's find a suitable place to have a quiet word with Gabriel."

The three gentlemen stood up as one putting on their sunglasses. The tall one left some money on the tea tray and exited with determined resolve. The other two dutifully followed him.

Frank and Ella were, as well, just about to leave the Cafe when WPC Knowle drew up a chair and sat down beside them. They were so engrossed with the three gentlemen that they completely failed to see the arrival of the policewoman into the cafe.

"Fancy meeting you two here on this special day. What a coincidence. I didn't think you thought much of unfortunate coincidences?"

"Good afternoon, WPC Knowle," said Frank in a pleasantly loud voice.

People on nearby tables shifted away from the policewoman. They were not used to the presence of the police force in the Mustard Seed Cafe.

"Good afternoon, Mr. and Mrs. Raleigh."

Ella offered "We did wonder why you were attending the funeral."

"Purely professional interest. There are a few loose ends that have been nagging me these past two weeks."

"Do you think it's murder?"

"No, it's probably not, but…"

Ella noticed a raising of an eyebrow.

"…I've been asked to gather more information before they decide whether to take an investigation any further."

Frank and Ella exchanged encouraging glances.

"However, I do know you two should not be here. You should not be taking such an interest in this death. It's none of your business."

"We know that but…" replied Frank.

However, Ella couldn't be contained.

"We think it was murder. If you don't think it's worth investigating, then it does no harm if we take an interest."

WPC Knowle almost smiled. "We're still undecided whether the incident is worth an investigation. I know, it's not against the law to snoop about. However, you must share any information with me!"

Frank and Ella exchanged another glance before Frank continued, "We drew up a list of four suspects!"

"We haven't decided yet whether it's a murder?"

Ella ignored the comment. "There's Agnes the ex-wife, Amelia the girlfriend, someone called Gabriel and a group of three very strange gentlemen who have just left this cafe."

"Ah, the Zummerzet Zyder Mafia!"

"Zyder Mafia?"

"Well, that's what they call themselves. What with the sunglasses and the black suits they're really getting into their roles. Pub landlords in this area don't like being intimidated by out of county people. The so-called Mafia are trying to persuade them to stock particular brands of Somerset Cider instead of the Devon cider that every landlord in the Sid

Valley sells. So far, they've had little success."

"Have they caused any trouble?"

"Not yet, but I'm aware of their presence. And our colleagues up in Taunton will be very supportive if any law-breaking ensues."

"Who do you think Gabriel might be?"

"Have you tried the pub next door to Billy Bowd's house?" The eyebrow was raised again.

Frank asked, "Are you trying to change the subject?"

"No!"

Ella ploughed on with the questions. "What time did Billy die?"

"Well, at a rough guess I would say three minutes past noon two Fridays ago!"

"Wow, that's incredibly precise. Normally, the pathologists on TV can only provide you with a range of about a couple of hours."

"Ah, but we're dealing in the real world. Modern science can be very precise. Especially, when we found his smashed watch. It had been broken when he fell. It stopped at three minutes past twelve!"

WPC Knowle looked at her watch and made as if to get up and leave.

Ella gripped his forearm. "Frank, darling, I think it's time we went. Go and settle the bill with that nice lady behind the counter. I'll wait for you outside."

"Right, goodbye WPC Knowle."

"Take care, both of you. And no snooping!"

The chairs and tables outside the Mariner Pub on River Street were unoccupied. There were no empty glasses or beer bottles. Frank sat down expecting Ella to follow suit. She went up to the front door, stared at it and then returned to Frank.

"Come on, let's take a walk along the seafront. I need to clear my head."

Frank got up frowning. However, he followed her and they walked in silence towards the promenade. This time they bypassed Taste.

"Why didn't you go into the pub?"

"Well, I looked at the licence details above the door and it said "Mr. Gabriel Metcombe. Licenced to sell all intoxicating liquor for consumption on or off these premises."

"So, that's our Gabriel. We could still have gone in."

"Well, he had company."

"Let me guess, the Zummerzet Zyder Mafia?"

"Absolutely spot on!"

They wandered along the promenade towards the lifeboat station lost in their thoughts. Yet again it was a beautiful clear day. Berry Head on the westerly side of Torbay was clearly visible.

"I suppose you're pleased now, aren't you?" An anguished shout destroyed their quiet contemplation.

Both Frank and Ella turned around to find Amelia rushing towards them.

"All that effort I put in, all that love and care. I tried my best to make him forget her. Then people like you come along and make him get all confused."

"Amelia, what are you talking about?"

"Don't you come all innocent with me. Everyone has the right to be stupid, but you are… abusing the privilege!"

"How dare you, young woman." Ella did not like Amelia's tone and aggressive stance.

"Oh yes, here you go again. Well, let me tell you, you're out of luck. Agnes and I, we got it all. She'll get the payout from the life insurance. I suppose, at least, she deserves it for putting up with him when she was his wife."

"What are you talking about?"

Amelia was in full flow. "Before the funeral, Agnes and I, we went to see the solicitor about the will. We're the closest he ever came to having a family. He's left me the house. I slept in it last night. On my own. It were strictly ghostly. I've never been more scared in my life. I think the 'ouse is being 'aunted by his ghost. I'd rather have the money. I ain't sleeping in that place ever again. His ghost will appear through the walls upside down with his legs in the air."

Frank and Ella were powerless to stop the torrent of words emanating from Amelia's befuddled brain.

"Perhaps I should get the life insurance as well. I could take Agnes for a walk up Salcombe Hill when I find her. I could demand the money from her. If she refuses me, then, I could take all of it! By fair means or foul! The cliffs are very high up there."

Ella recovered the power of speech. "Amelia, you're not making any sense. Have you been drinking?"

"Huh, very soon there may well be two deaths in the family."

Amelia spat on the ground at Ella's feet and turned and waddled away from them in a hasty but haphazard fashion. She turned her head back towards them and screamed, "I'm going for a walk up Salcombe Hill with Agnes... so I can throw her off the cliff!"

Without hesitation, she darted across the road, narrowly avoiding being flattened by a passing car. A screeching of tyres and the decibelistic sound of the car horn caused most of the promenade to gaze in her direction to see what caused the cacophony.

Amelia glared menacingly at the driver. The driver appealed to the heavens above and slapped his hands on his steering wheel. Non-verbal communication ensued between the two of them as Amelia continued on her zig-zagging way.

Ella, meanwhile, was flushed and flustered. "That woman is the rudest and most baffling creature in the whole Sid Valley. She's my chief suspect!"

"I'm not so sure. At least, she told us some more information." Frank took Ella's hand as he turned to face her. "There is a will, and the money is going to Agnes, and the house is going to her!"

"Lucky them!"

"Do you think, she's really going for that walk?"

"I don't think she would get halfway up the hill before collapsing. I do think, however, that she's cracking up under the strain of it all. It could get rather messy!"

CHAPTER SEVEN

IT'S HEAVEN IN DEVON

Solvitur ambulando 1

Frank and Ella sat at home drinking coffee and staring out over Mutter's Moor. The early morning cloud had cleared away and the whole length of the tree-lined hillside was crisply visible. The breeze had died down. Yet again, there was hardly a cloud in the sky.

"You know, Frank, it's a beautiful morning. We need to get away from this detective work. My mind is buzzing with a multitude of theories!"

"Clear our heads?"

"Exactly! What about a walk? Let's go somewhere on the Coast Path and just blow away the cobwebs, forget all about our problems and enjoy this glorious autumn weather."

"Where do you want to go?"

"Somewhere around here."

Frank went to his laptop, opened his Firefox browser and quickly found the South West Coast Path website. He typed Sidmouth into the walk finder. Twenty walks appeared on the Walk Finder page. He dismissed the seven easy and three challenging walks. Ten moderate walks remained.

Frank scrolled down the list. "Salcombe Hill? Otterton Mill? The Donkey Sanctuary Walk?"

"No, all too far away."

"Mutter's Moor and Peak Hill?"

"That's more like it."

Ella come over and looked over his shoulder at the walk description.

"It's not the Coast Path, but we've never walked up on Mutter's Moor."

She went and sat back down in her favourite chair facing out of the window towards their very own Mutter's Moor view.

"How far is this walk?"

"Just over three miles. We'll take the car to the Mutter's Moor car park."

"What does it say about the route?"

Frank read from the walk description.

"A walk through prehistory, following ancient tracks through an area thought to be densely populated in the Stone Age. There are breathtaking views in every direction and an abundance of wildlife in the colourful heathland. Children will love the freedom of the open space, as well as the tales of smugglers and cavemen. A good walk for autumn, when birds raid the bushes for berries and the heath is bright with heather and gorse."

"Well, we haven't got our children with us anymore but it is still autumn, so it sounds perfect. Take your phone and we can check for directions if we get lost!"

"The route looks straightforward and level! It goes along the heathland to just above Newton Poppleford. Then we take a brief circle and retrace our steps back to the car park."

"We could walk and then pop down to the Connaught Gardens. We could stop at the Clock Tower cafe for lunch."

"Great idea. We leave in 15 minutes!"

"Aye-aye, Captain!"

The morning was perfect. The car park was surprisingly half-full. They avoided as many of the bumps and ruts as they could and parked under the swaying branches of a conifer tree. They laced up their walking boots. According to the weather forecast, wet weather gear was not needed. Frank locked the car and off they set.

They headed inland away from the sea. The track was wide and flat with evergreen trees on one side and heathland bracken on the other. A variety of birds added their extensive range of tuneful melody.

"What a lovely place," Ella was already convinced they had made the correct choice to walk on Mutter's Moor.

The web browser on Frank's phone was open at the Mutter's Moor walk page on the South West Coast Path website. Frank had saved the walk description so that it was readable in offline mode. Now and again, without Ella's awareness, Frank would innocently drop in some morsel of relevant knowledge.

"How do you know all this?"

"I'm a good reader!" Frank held up the phone and laughed.

"Did you know that we're walking on one of Europe's oldest and largest pebble-bed heaths?"

"So knowledgeable!"

"It's owned by Clinton Devon Estates. In 1930, Lord Clinton opened it up to the general public for air and exercise!"

"That, O great mastermind, was an excellent decision!"

"It was once seven separate commons."

"One for every day of the week."

At regular intervals, dogs with and without their owners passed them by. A cheery "Good Morning!" from the owners was met with genuine smiles and words of reply.

One thing both Frank and Ella noticed when moving into the area was how people would actually take the time to talk to you. No heads were buried in a phone or counting the cracks in the pavement. Up here it helped that there were no pavements and intermittent mobile phone reception, but still, people talked to you!

Frank continued to prove his reading ability was not diminished by his advancing age. "Did you know the Baron of Clinton was a title bestowed in 1299, the second oldest barony in Britain?"

"Barony, what sort of a word is that? Do you mean baloney?"

Frank's voice was full of magisterial authority. "Barony is a very high-ranking word!"

"Yes, and a baron ranks above all knighthoods. You address a baron as Sir!"

"Have you got your phone open as well?"

"No, some of us retain information in our brains, not our mobiles!"

The heathland's bracken, its heather and the mounds of rough grass were home to insects, moths, butterflies and lizards- even the shy adder. Frank and Ella saw none of these, even at this time of year. They did spot a buzzard flying lazily and gracefully high above them on the lookout for suitable prey.

They were in no hurry and they often stopped to take in the stunning views over towards the South Devon coast. At certain stages of the walk, they were able to enjoy the southern end of the Otter Valley stretching down to Budleigh Salterton and then beyond to the Exe Valley estuary at Exmouth and Dawlish Warren. Their eyes could follow the coastline past Teignmouth and down towards Torbay. Even Berry Head beyond Brixham was clearly visible.

"It's heaven in Devon," Ella sighed.

Eventually, the walk curved around, and they made their way back to the car park. There, they crossed the road and wandered over the rough grassland to the cliff edge of Peak Hill. From here the South West Coast Path headed downhill eastwards towards Sidmouth and westwards to Ladram Bay and its famous sea-stacks. They sat on the shorter grass by the path and once more enjoyed the glorious views towards Berry Head. Dartmoor was visible on the horizon on the other side of the Exe Valley. Even at this time of the year, walkers both casual and long-distance passed them by. A large percentage of them taking the time to stop and admire the view before venturing downhill.

What wind there was blew in from the sea. They followed the paths of a few fishing boats making their way slowly parallel to the coast. A helicopter flew low overhead as it followed the coastline from Exmouth. It disappeared into the distance as it headed for Seaton and Lyme Regis. Seagulls, refugees from Sidmouth, occasionally appeared from below the clifftop as they flew upwards on the air currents before soaring above the red cliffs.

All good things come to an end and in just over two hours after the start of their walk they were back at the car, refreshed, revitalised and ready to enjoy some lunch down in Sidmouth at the Connaught Gardens.

CHAPTER EIGHT

NOTHING TOO RISKY BUT NOTHING TOO LEGAL

Every man at the bottom of his heart believes that he is a born detective.

Lunch at the Clock Tower Cafe in the Connaught Gardens was superb as usual. The sound of the sea hitting the rocks below Jacob's Ladder, the ever-present squawking of the seagulls, the clink of cups and saucers and the soft murmur of subdued conversation added to the ambient delight.

Frank and Ella's Ploughman's were finally and fully devoured. Ella broached the topic that neither really wanted to discuss.

"Well, do we continue or just walk away?"

"A bit late if you're meaning the meal? We've both just finished!"

"You know exactly what I mean! Our investigation, if that's what it is, into Cidered of Sidmouth."

"Very good phrase! Well, WPC Knowle told us to mind our own business, but I'm quite interested to find out as much as we can. We can always pass on our findings to her at the appropriate time!"

"I was so hoping you'd say that! We both read so many detective books that it would be a shame to just walk away when we have a real live murder opening up before our very eyes!"

"I don't think you can have a real live murder?"

"Oxymoron?"

"Definitely maybe!"

A smirk appeared on Frank's face. "Right, if we're going to investigate, we need a plan of action."

"In Death in Paradise, they always write everything up on a whiteboard."

"We haven't got a whiteboard," Frank chuckled.

"We've got a corkboard in the garage. We could cover that with stiff paper!"

"We'll list our suspects, their motives and then find a way to meet with them and find out as much as we can in a cautious and discrete manner."

"If we both put one of those dictaphone recording apps on our phones then we can record any conversations. We may even be able to use them as evidence."

"Isn't that some breach of the law?"

"It takes a thief to catch a thief! The detective and his criminal wear versions of the same mask."

"Good quote."

"Jane Roberts. Now she was a very strange personality. She was an American who channelled this person called Seth."

"Wasn't she the one who said, "You create your own reality"?"

"Absolutely!" beamed Ella.

"That was a real new age phrase that the mass media loved!"

They both sat there drinking in the gentle surroundings. The flower beds were just being dug over, ready for their winter hibernation. The grass was still a bright and lively green. The crazy paving pathways were devoid of weeds and moss. They could hear the birds in the nearby trees to their left and the gentle swish of the sea on their right.

"We couldn't do this if we were still working?"

Ella thought that there may be something in this retirement after all.

"Let's get home, put up the whiteboard, create our own reality and solve a murder!"

The whiteboard was quickly constructed. Frank wrote Suspect, Motive, Alibi and Notes across the top of the paper leaving lots of space for the latter heading. He then drew lines down the paper dividing the headings into columns. The Notes column was four times the width of each of the other three.

Ella took over and spaced out down the left-hand side the names of the suspects.

"Amelia has to be the first name!" She immediately wrote in that name.

"Fair enough, but then add Agnes straight underneath."

"Then there's Gabriel Metcombe at the Mariners pub."

Ella tried to keep the handwriting both legible and neat. All these names were on there for the long run.

Frank remembered, "The Zummerzet Zyder Mafia?"

"Yes, not very likely but sometimes the most unlikely end up being our murderers."

Silence filled the room. Serious thinking time.

Ella dredged up from somewhere, "Steer clear of 'arry!"

"Pardon?"

"That's what they said. Steer clear of 'arry."

"Yes, you're right. I remember the Mafia said that in the cafe."

"Who's 'Arry?"

I don't know yet but put him or her down as well."

Ella finished writing. "That's five suspects that we know about."

They both thought for a while.

"Wait a minute," Ella continued, "What about where Billy worked? Sowden Valley Cider Farm up near Clyst St Lawrence, you said."

"Yes, what if he had enemies in his workplace? He wouldn't be the first."

"There could be any number of suspects there. I'm putting them down as well." She wrote "Unknown fellow workers."

"And then there's A.N.Other! It could be somebody we know nothing about. A random burglar. A person out of his past."

"Wow, the list is growing ever longer by the minute."

Frank nodded, "I think we need to speak to all of them, bit by bit, one by one.

"All the ones we can speak to! A.N.Other might be hard to find!"

"True, then we share our thoughts with WPC Knowle and see if she has any other suspects on the horizon."

After a brief moment of contemplation, Ella said, "We need to find out more about Billy's life. Who were his friends? What did he do at work? What did he do out of work?"

"The more we find out about him the better our chances of discovering how and why he died."

Companionable silence filled the room once more. Then

finally, Frank took the whiteboard pen and wrote Money in the Motive column alongside Agnes' name.

"Absolutely! Ditto for Amelia." Ella said. She considered that for a moment before adding, "They both could have easily killed for the money. But, shouldn't you add in love as well? Either of them may well have been jealous. It could have been a crime of passion."

"True, the front room and the bedroom certainly looked a mess."

Frank wrote in the motive column Jealousy and then Love alongside both their names.

"Next?"

"The Mafia are meant to be after business in the Sid Valley. Perhaps they wanted to let everyone know what would happen if they didn't come on board the Zummerzet Zyder train!"

Frank laughed. "You've been watching the Godfather again."

"Let's not get personal. What about the pub landlord?"

"Perhaps he had a business deal with him and it went wrong or maybe the landlord had an affair with Billy's ex-wife. They lived next door."

Ella nodded as Frank added the words Business Deal and Affair into the motive column. She looked down the list of suspects. "Fellow-workers?"

"Jealousy? Blackmail? Revenge? Hatred?"

Frank wrote further words into the motive column and then put down the pen.

"Enough talking. We need to put our ideas into action. Let's see if Gabriel Metcombe at the Mariner's has finished his conversation with the Zummerzet Zyder Mafia yet."

Gabriel was in the Mariner's Pub when Frank and Ella walked into the saloon bar. No-one else was there. Gabriel was sat slumped in a window seat behind a fake antique table, staring sullenly out of the window. He looked about sixty, maybe even slightly older. There was no way he could be described as the George Clooney of Sidmouth. Unkempt hair thinning on top, unkempt clothes, a jersey with a distinct hole in one sleeve. Trousers that were beer-stained and an ugly shade of grey. However, despite that, something was troubling him. Both Frank and Ella had a pretty good guess what it might be.

He rose as they moved towards him. He struggled for a smile which he just about achieved. "Good afternoon my lovelies, what can I get you?"

"Some cider, please. Do you sell Sowden Valley here?"

"No, we don't. I don't think I've ever 'eard of it."

Ella raised an eyebrow expressing her disbelief in his answer. "Really, that's not what we've been told."

"What do you mean?"

"Well, you know Billy Bowd? Your next-door neighbour?"

"Now that were a terrible business. Terrible. I thought it would bring lots of extra customers through my doors. You know people are always drawn to the scene of a death. But, as you can see, it seems to have 'ad opposite effect."

He waved his hand at the empty room.

"Quite. However, we know about you and Billy and your little game, Mr. Metcombe."

Gabriel's face dissolved in shock.

"How d'yer find out?" he blustered. His troubled demeanour quickly came back to the surface, "I thought we were discrete."

"Not discrete enough."

"No, you're probably right."

There was an embarrassing pause in the conversation. Gabriel didn't seem to want to try too hard to conceal the truth. He looked resigned to his fate. Ella was sure she could see tears in the old man's eyes.

So she took the plunge. "You can tell us all about it. We know you didn't mean it."

"Too darn right. It's been driving me billid for months now. It's wrong and if I were found out, I'd lose my licence and this pub. Fifteen years of my life I've put into this place. I don't want to lose it now. And all over some cut-price cider."

"So you admit you had an arrangement with Billy?"

"Yes, he managed to get me a small and steady supply of the drink. He brought some out of the yard most days. I don't understand how he never got found out. Stored it in that gert big cider barrel of his in the courtyard. Drip feed, he said."

Gabriel almost looked grateful to be able to put into words the secret deception he had been hiding away for so long.

"I knew it were wrong, but I still sold it. I called it Special 'oniton Select. I charged customers twenty-five per cent higher than my other brands. Even my regulars loved it. Because it were more expensive, they thought it were best quality. It were easy profit."

"Have you been able to get any more of this cider?"

"Naw, not a chance. Billy were my sole supplier. I weren't going to touch the rest of that cider in the barrel next door. Dead man's blood and cider don't mang too well with customers."

Frank smiled and changed the subject. "What was Billy like?"

Gabriel looked off towards the small cider barrels on the bar and almost smiled. "Like a Sweet Coppin. He liked 'is bibble. He always reminds, er, reminded me of that character in that Dad's Army program they keep showing on the TV."

"Private Walker?"

"Yes, a Devonian version of Private Walker. Always looking out for a chance to make easy money. Nothing too risky but nothing too legal."

"Did he make any enemies?"

"No, that were the most crazed thing. He had that cheeky, cheery smile on his face. People loved him, even when they knew he were cheating them. How he got away with it for so long, I don't know. He never hurt anyone physically but, boy, he could try your patience. He were the living embodiment of Devon Time. He did things in his own way in his own time. People called him infuriating!"

"Well, he must have pushed someone too far. Someone ran out of patience."

Ella added, "How patient are you, Mr. Metcombe?"

"How patient? I have my days, I s'pose!"

"Did you have an argument? Did he up his price? Did he perhaps want to sell his ill-gotten drink to some other pub?"

"Here, wait a minute. Are you suggesting I 'ad something to do with his death? 'Ow dare 'ee. You may be my only customers this afternoon, but I won't be serving 'ee. Get out. If 'ee breathe one word of this conversation to anybody then I'll be denying every word. If 'ee go to the police or the licensing people then watch out. We won't be wanting another murder in Sidmouth, will we?"

"So, you think Billy was murdered?"

"Get out this instant or this time it'll be a double murder. I'm closing and neither you nor 'er be welcome here any longer."

Gabriel raised himself up from his window seat and menacingly moved towards them. Both Frank and Ella rapidly left the Mariners feeling the interview needed to be terminated on Health and Safety grounds. Their Health and their Safety!

Outside in the Autumn sunlight, both Frank and Ella walked quickly to Blackmore Gardens checking they hadn't been followed. They sat on a bench near the bandstand before reaching into their pockets for their phones. They both pressed the stop button on their voice recording apps.

"Well, that was illuminating!" uttered Frank.

CHAPTER NINE

PRAPER DEB'N WAY

The probability of someone watching you is proportional to the stupidity of your actions.

"He lied to us right at the start of our conversation."

Ella nodded in agreement "So how many other times did he lie? I'm thinking seriously now about changing my number one suspect. I felt threatened by him. I'm certain that he could have killed us if he got angry enough!"

"I'm not sure about that but we need to make copies of our recordings and then transcribe them. He was a real Devonian, wasn't he? I'll need to do some research to find out what some of his words mean!"

They made for home and spent the evening copying and transcribing their recordings. Frank found a couple of useful internet sites that helped him translate the Devonian dialect into the Queen's English.

After an hour or so, Frank sat back from his computer and appeared smugly pleased with his research. "There are only four words I didn't understand but this website translates billid as meaning mad, Mang means to mix, bibble is to drink too much and Sweet Coppin is a variety of Cider Apple."

"That makes a little more sense of the conversation. I'll have to look out for Sweet Coppin. I wonder if they're eating or cooking apples as well."

"Could you get drunk eating cider apples?" Frank was strictly a special occasions drinker and then only enough to be sociable.

"Talking of apples, why don't we go tomorrow and visit the Sowden Valley Cider Farm. Clyst St Lawrence is not too far from here." Ella was all fired up now. Life was becoming more and more interesting as each day unfolded.

The next day the rain poured down in bucket-loads from a grey cloudy sky.

"We're not going to let a bit of rain stop us?" taunted Ella.

"Actually, I agree. There's more chance that the manager will be warm and dry in his office rather than getting soaked going around and about the farm!"

They reached Sowden Valley and found a bedraggled worker squelching through the puddles towards a muddy and battered old quad bike. It had a trailer filled to the brim with aromatic bags of manure. As the worker climbed on, Frank wound down his window and asked politely, "Where can I find the owner?"

Bedraggled stuck his thumb out in the direction of a small building adjacent to a barn. "All cosy and varm in there!"

He then loudly roared off in the direction of the orchard.

"Do you know you can take one of those things on the roads these days?" Frank said when the quad bike had disappeared into the orchard.

"Well, you won't ever find me riding on one of them, ever. Too noisy."

Frank and Ella parked their car as close to the building as possible and made for the wooden door. Frank knocked loudly and without waiting for an answer pushed open the door and walked in.

"I told you just now which of them Sweet Coppins need checking. I let you use my quad to go into Cullompton and…"

"Good morning," Ella butted in.

"Oh, sorry, ma'am," I thought you were that idiot Metcombe coming in to avoid a little mizzle."

"Mizzle? It's pouring down!"

"Yes, maybe in London, but this is definitely mizzle."

Ella looked out of the office window at the puddles in the yard widening by the minute.

"Do you sell your cider here? We couldn't see a shop on our way in."

"No, not yet. It's one of the many things on my to-do list. If you want our best cider there are a few select pubs in Cullompton, Tiverton and Honiton."

"Oh, we live near Sidmouth. Any in Sidmouth?"

"No, not yet. I'm waiting for my so-called foreman cum sales director to arrive. He should have been getting Sowden Valley Cider into a couple of pubs in Sidmouth but he's a lazy meech. He's not been here for a few weeks now. I think he's gone walkabout."

"Is that Billy Bowd?"

"Yes, how did you know?"

"Well, he won't be in today or any other day for that matter."

"What's he been up to now? I'm getting fed up with his shenanigans and his wheeling and dealing. The minute he shows his pretty face back in here, I'll turn him right round and whop him off my farm."

"You won't be able to whop him off your farm or any other place for that matter."

"Why not?"

"He's dead!" Frank watched for the shock to appear on the manager's face. It took a few seconds for him to register what Frank had told him.

"Dead? How? When?"

Ella gave him an extremely brief potted version of the day when they discovered his body.

"We were delivering a package that had been misdirected to our house. Posted from Cullompton way. We knocked and no-one answered. We found the key under the flowerpot and went in to leave the package on the kitchen table. We found him in the back courtyard. In the cider barrel headfirst with his legs sticking out."

"In the courtyard? With his feet sticking out of that huge Cider Vat? What a tragic accident!"

"That's exactly what the police said."

"Well, they should know. They probably deal with lots of suicides or accidents all the time. Poor old Billy Bowd."

There was an uncomfortable silence. They could hear the rain tapping on the corrugated roof of the office.

"I never introduced myself, did I? I'm Harry Sowden, the manager and owner of the Sowden Valley Farm. We aim to be the finest specialist cider makers in the whole of the West Country!"

"Yes, I'm Frank, Frank Raleigh and this is my wife, Ella."

"No relation to Sir Walter?" Harry's face almost creased into the first smile of the day.

"No, not as far as we know!" Ella noticed a lessening of the tension that had been steadily building ever since they had entered the office. However, she wasn't giving up her detective work that easily.

"What was Billy like here at work?" she asked. "We met a few of his friends and acquaintances and they say he was a cheeky fly by night."

"Why do you want to know?"

"Well, after finding him in the Cider barrel, we felt kind of sorry for him. Did he deserve to die like that?"

Frank's attention began to waver. He wondered how long the rain would continue. He didn't particularly like driving in wet weather.

"Don't feel sorry for him. He was cheeky, as you say. And when he first came here, he was a good worker. But that didn't last long. He became lazy, slippery and... I shouldn't tell you this. It'll make you want to forget all about feeling sorry for him."

Harry's almost smile vanished as quickly as it had appeared. Frank paid attention once more.

Ella was sitting over by the window out of the manager's sight-line. She surreptitiously switched on her phone's voice recording app. Why hadn't she done that before they came into the office?

"He was blackmailing me... or trying to. Said he had copied down the secret recipe we use to make our top-quality brand of cider-Sowden Valley Select."

"Blackmail?"

"And he said he'd sell it to the highest bidder. I didn't believe him but that didn't stop him. I was going to pay him a little bonus and then sack him."

"What was to stop him still selling the recipe?"

"Nothing, but I don't think he had the recipe. It's not just the ingredients, it's how the apples are stored, how and when they are ground, how many times the pomace is pressed. The whole process."

"How fascinating," blurted Ella, "I never knew so much went into making cider."

"Yes, we've been making cider the praper Deb'n way for years. First of all, as just a hobby. Then local people started telling us they praper loved our cider. So we've started making more. Not much money in it, but it keeps us afloat. If we lost the recipe and others replicated our manufacturing process, we'd be bankrupt in a couple of years. The Zummerzet Mafia would have the facilities to replicate our manufacturing process. They'd kill for the recipe."

"Kill?" Ella looked shocked.

"Well, maybe not kill. But they'd be very interested in acquiring any information about how Sowden Valley Select is made."

"So Billy Bowd's death could be a blessing for you?" Frank awaited a reaction.

"Now that's a nasty thing to say. I take no pleasure in the manner of our blessing! It's a tragedy that Billy's dead. Despite everything, no -one deserved such a fate."

There was a moment of silence whilst Harry considered his next words.

"I also think he was stealing some of the cider. Bottles went missing on a regular basis. Never too many at any one time but over the months, a great deal of high-quality cider. My high-quality cider!"

"Did you ever confront him? Here on the farm?"

"I was going to have it out with him when he returned to work."

"I'd have thought you would go after him rather than just waiting."

"Did you go to his house?" Ella interjected.

"Never did."

"Do you know where Billy lived?"

"No, somewhere near Sidmouth. I'd have to look it up in his personnel file."

"No, there's no need to put yourself to any extra work."

"It's no bother. But I steer clear of Sidmouth. I don't like seaside places. I prefer the countryside."

"So you've never been to Sidmouth?"

"Don't be silly! Course I been there. But not for a year or more. Last summer for the Folk Festival. Tried to sell some of my cider. But I didn't have the right sort of licence then. I didn't bother going back this year."

Ella thought that he gave them far more information than she was expecting him to provide.

"Anyway - what day did you say he died?"

"I didn't."

"Oh, I thought you wanted to know if he was here on that day?"

Frank told him. Harry hastily consulted a battered diary on his desk. "Well, on that day, I was in Barnstaple. At the Pannier market. Selling Cider. And Billy was nowhere to be found. Again."

Ella and Frank moved towards the door of the office and prepared to venture out into the mizzle once more.

"Wait a moment. If you're interested, I've got a spare half an hour as it's still mizzling. I could take you around the barn and show you how Sowden Valley Select is made. I'm sure I could even organise a taster session."

Frank and Ella stopped and smiled warmly at their host.

"That sounds scrummy," said Ella.

"Scrumpy? Very good!" snickered Harry. The almost-smile re-appeared.

They stood in the doorway of the office looking out over one of the orchards.

"We base our whole process on the groundbreaking work of Sir John Heathcoat up at Heathcoat Amory farm in Lythecourt near Tiverton."

"Oh, does he make good cider?"

"The best. Or, at least, his farm did. He died just before the First World War. Cider was made at Lythecourt's Home Farm - pure unadulterated cider. We follow their method most assiduously."

"Fascinating!" Ella was a sucker for a good historical yarn.

"We keep our orchards in tip-top condition. Well-pruned, no canker, grease bands around the trunks to stop moths laying eggs in the branches. We make sure that light and air get to the fruit by pruning away most of the moss and lichen. We get rid of the rest of it the old-fashioned way, with powdered lime on the branches on a wet still winter's day."

"Do you use special varieties of apples?"

"No, any apples will do. It's how you treat them that's important. We grow Billy Down Pippin and Fair Maid of Devon varieties but so do lots of other farms."

Harry gazed out at the grey sky. It was still raining. He picked up an umbrella from behind the door.

"We pick the orchards three times. The last time we give the trees a real shaking down so that we get all the apples. We separate these windfalls from the other gatherings. Only the first gathering is used for the Select cider. The rest we use to make ordinary cider. We sell most of that to the supermarkets. Their customers never notice the difference, but we do!"

Harry opened his umbrella and held it out over Ella and himself.

"Follow me to the barn. It's only next door. We won't get too wet!"

Ella and Harry stayed dry whilst Frank followed behind attempting to walk between the raindrops.

They stood just inside the barn.

"All the apples are stored off the ground under cover in our granary. They can keep that way for about a month or more without heating or rotting. We ground them before they get rotten."

Harry started walking into the barn pointing at the walls and roof.

"You can see that the barn is well ventilated and light. We still whitewash the walls. The apple pomace is thrown into that shute over there which leads to the cage-press. We press them there and pump the juice into one of those large vats over there. They hold 200 gallons each. The pomace is pressed again in the next power press but the juice is not the same quality. We pump that into that massive blending vat in the corner. That holds over 1,000 gallons. We only fill them up to about a foot from the top. We call the process keeving. The vats have removable covers. We skim the head off the vats maybe three or four times. We end up with a naturally sweet, well coloured and brilliantly clear cider."

"Is the cider ready for drinking then?" Ella was captivated by the whole process.

"No, it's on to the filtration. We force the cider through the filter, but not too fast."

"Why?"

"It'll diminish the flavour. That's why you can't just follow the recipe. It's almost an art. Sometimes the juice will go through the filter the day it is pressed, other times we need to wait. The filtered juice goes by those pipes to the casks down there."

Harry pointed to what appeared to be an open cellar in the floor.

"Those casks are steam washed before being filled. As soon as it is filled, the cask is bunged down. We insert a tube into the bung to take away any carbonic acid that is given off by the fermenting cider."

"Very impressive," said Frank, genuinely amazed by the clear description of the complex process.

"Yes, it is," said Harry. "We try to ferment the cider as slowly as possible through the winter before bottling it in April. The cider should be clear and absolutely brilliant before bottling. If we get it right, then bottled cider will keep and improve for several years."

"Just like wine?"

"Exactly. We've found that the old-fashioned way produces the very best cider. You'll not taste any better cider in the whole West Country, including Zummerzet!"

"There's a great deal of skill in every part of the process."

"Yes, not everybody can make great cider. We can. We do."

Frank and Ella were treated to a small sampling of last year's vintage. It was delightfully, brilliantly clear and sweet tasting. It was the colour of yellow harvest, the taste of sweet summer apples.

"Time to go."

"Yeah, you don't want to get apple-pied."

"Thanks for the tour," Ella said, "I hope you sort out your cider marketing problems."

"Cheers."

They made their way back to the car.

"Are you sure you're all right to drive?"

"Ella, I only had a sip. I know my responsibilities."

"I believe you. Why don't we go into Cullompton and see if we can buy a few bottles of Sowden Valley Select? It'll make a nice change from our usual cup of water at dinner."

Ella took her phone out to switch off the recording app only to discover her phone battery was down to one per cent. The app had turned itself off automatically.

"Well, I'll be clotted!" she cried.

Frank looked at her. Ella looked at Frank. They both burst out laughing.

"You're becoming a local yokel, speaking like that!"

"Sorry, Frank, it just came out of nowhere. I turned my phone app on to record the conversation and the battery's run out. I don't know how much it recorded. Did I miss something? He seemed to be willing to give out far more information than we wanted to know!"

"Yes, I thought that as well. We'll check on the recording when we get home."

"Could he be our 'Arry? The one they said to steer clear of?"

"It wouldn't surprise me. If he is, at least, he's got an alibi."

"He seemed very determined to let us know where he was on the day of the murder."

"Hope that wasn't a guilty conscience. I quite liked him."

Frank started the car engine and they drove off away from Sowden Valley Farm. After a mile or so, the farm was already far behind them when Ella reminded Frank about going into Cullompton to find some of that Select Cider.

"Just for a little background research, of course!"

"Naturally, what other reason?"

"Well, I fancy some lunch. Don't you?"

"A good old fashioned roast dinner."

"In the middle of the week?"

"Doesn't matter. We're retired with nothing else to do so why not?"

"Nothing else to do. We're rapidly becoming full-time detectives."

As they drove over the M5 and approached Cullompton, Frank began ruminating over the early part of their meeting with Harry.

"You know, I don't think we were very good detectives back in the farm office."

"Why?"

"Well, we told him as much as he told us. Next time we need to speak much less, listen a lot more and concentrate. We need to ask open-ended questions. It's a bit like being a teacher once again."

Ella nodded. "I know what you mean. We used to get the youngsters to exercise their thinking skills and not just copying everything we say parrot fashion."

"Let their thoughts flow and who knows what they'll reveal."

"Right. I'm willing to learn from my mistakes."

"Same here."

They were in Cullompton now. Ella pointed at a pub coming up on her left. "Let's stop here. It looks cosy and the board outside is advertising roasts every day."

They struck lucky. The pub was cosy. Warm and cosy. It served an excellent lunch of roast beef and Yorkshire pudding with all the trimmings. And they stocked the cider they had heard so much about during the morning. Frank wasn't sure how potent Sowden Valley Select would be, so they bought a couple of bottles to take home and sample later. In the pub, he stayed with the orange juice and lemonade.

The meal over and a reasonable bill paid, they climbed back in their car and decided to take the A373, the quiet road to Honiton rather than use the motorway to go back home.

After a couple of gentle miles, Frank frowned, "That's strange."

"What?"

"Well, there's an old rusty Land Rover behind us. I swear he was behind us on the way into Cullompton. I think we might be being followed."

"Why?"

"I don't know. I'm going to take a right here. Signposted Luton and Clyst William."

They turned off the Honiton road.

Ella checked in her wing mirror. "They've turned off as well. Could just be an unfortunate coincidence."

"OK. Let's go through Luton and head for Payhembury."

Frank kept a watchful eye on their followers in his rear-view mirror. Ella kept her gaze on the wing mirror. "They're still behind us. Frank, I don't like this."

Then she screamed, "Watch out!!"

Frank was confronted by a large tractor towing a muck spreader manoeuvring itself around the approaching t-junction. The road was only wide enough for one vehicle. Frank skidded to a halt, swerved onto the grass and narrowly avoided scratches from the overhanging hedges. He missed the tractor by what seemed like millimetres and slid back on to the narrow winding road.

The tractor was slower to react and stumbled to a standstill some 10 metres later blocking the whole road. The rusty Land Rover screeched to a halt and despite a cacophony of horn blasts, was forced to reverse. The front seat passenger wound down his window and shouted "Stop! Wait! Stop!"

Ella turned to Frank. "I don't think so. Drive on whilst they're stuck."

Frank sped onwards towards the main road. When he reached

it, he turned left back towards Cullompton. He sped up when the road was straight, took the corners and bends as quickly but as carefully as he dared. It wasn't a road for overtaking, very few Devon roads are. There were too many occasions when they were travelling too slowly for their liking.

"Must be the slowest car chase ever!" scrawled Ella.

Frank was too busy checking the rear-view mirror.

"Still behind us. A couple of cars back but still behind."

"What do we do now?"

"Well, we could stop and confront them. Or we could head to the motorway and try to lose them. This car is surely faster than an old Land Rover."

Ella's face had turned paler than usual but there was a steely determination in her voice. "I hope we don't regret this but let's lose them on the motorway."

"How many in the Land Rover? It looks like three of them?"

Ella tried to use the wing mirror but with the speed they were travelling at, it was shaking and wobbling all over the place.

"It's difficult to be sure. I think, there's three. There's definitely two, the driver and a front seat companion. It looks like there's just one in the back. They're all wearing sunglasses. On a day like today!!"

They reached the junction that led down to the motorway. The M5 had its usual share of lorries and vans. Frank weaved a bit around a couple of large lorries before heading for the outside lane.

With a cry of "Geronimo!" he put his foot down. The car responded and soon reached triple figures. It didn't feel that fast until Ella glanced out of the window at the crash barrier posts flashing by her.

In no time at all, Frank was pulling off the motorway at Junction 30. Thankfully, he had driven the eleven miles without attracting the attention of the traffic police.

"I've never driven so fast before in my life. And I don't want to ever again!" Frank breathed an enormous sigh of relief that they had left the motorway and were still in one piece. However, he was forced to wait, for what appeared to be forever, at the traffic lights at the foot of the slip-road.

"Come on, change!"

"Can I open my eyes now?" Ella looked over at Frank. He was sweating. She looked in her passenger windshield mirror. She was still a whiter shade of pale.

The car now appeared to be travelling really slowly as they settled into the usual 40mph on the A3052. They were headed for home.

"Frank?"

"Yes?"

"They're still behind us. About three cars back."

"Oh no, I thought we'd lost them. Right, I think it's time to put Plan B into action."

"I hope it's less scary than Plan A."

"Let's wait and see. It involves a little bit of a confrontation."

"Oh, go for it, I'm right beside you!"

Without warning, Frank turned sharp left off the main road towards a village signposted Farringdon. At a convenient passing place, he screeched to a halt.

CHAPTER TEN

CLEARING AWAY THE COBWEBS

Solvitur ambulando 2

The rusty Land Rover appeared chugging as fast as it could along the hedge-lined lane. Thankfully for everyone at the scene, it stumbled to a wheezing halt.

Frank got out of the car and marched towards the Land Rover. He leant against the driver's door and hammered was his clenched fist forcefully on the window.

Ella joined him on the other side of the car just as the passenger opened the door. She slammed it shut catching him on the knees. A rather obvious swear word emanated from the passenger's mouth.

The driver successfully wound down his window.

"Don't you dare move. Stay in this rust bucket and start talking. Why are you trying to scare my wife half to death?"

Frank recognised the three occupants immediately in spite of, or because of, the sunglasses.

"You drive very fast for an old'un!" The driver tried a smile, but it was obviously fake.

"You're a long way from Taunton!"

"That's a good 'un!" came a cry from the back seat, "Down from Taunton like a grockel on a jolly."

"Why are you following us and endangering our lives?"

"We just wanted to ask you a few questions." The driver looked up at Frank with a fake news smile on his face.

His front-seat passenger leaned across and added, "We don't mean you any harm."

The driver continued, "We tried to flag you down in Cullompton. I flashed my lights at you so many times. You must have seen us! You were the one driving like a bat out of hell down the M5."

"You scared us! We were trying to escape from you!" Ella joined in the conversation from around the other side of the Land Rover.

"You're lying about the lights. We didn't see your headlights flashing once, let alone 'so many times'!"

The front passenger turned to speak to the occupant in the back seat. "Delbert, I told you to check the lights last night. Now both bulbs have gone. This is a disaster of a vehicle. We need something much better than this - what did he call it? - rust bucket!"

"Never a truer word was spoken," agreed the driver.

The front seat passenger started to dominate the conversation. "Well, I'm sorry about that. It seems we weren't having any success in attracting your attention. Still, no harm was done."

"No harm done?" blustered Ella.

The front seat passenger waited for the echo of Ella's words to fade away. "What we wanted to ask you is simply this. We love Sowden Valley Select. However, Harry Sowden doesn't want his recipe to go outside of Devon. Furthermore, seeing we're affectionately known as the Zummerzet Zyder Mafia by the licenced victuallers here in Devon, he won't sell to us."

"You haven't asked your question yet!" said Frank.

"Yes, you're quite correct, of course. Well, it's this. Have you been bidding for the recipe? If Harry sells his recipe to you, we'll match your price and add on twenty-five per cent."

"Why would Harry sell to us?"

"That's why you were there this morning, wasn't it? To bid for the Sowden Valley Select recipe? Do you work for one of the Devon Cider companies?"

"Well, that's for you to find out. But the price would be at least double, not a measly twenty-five per cent!"

A voice piped up from the back seat, "Seems fair enough. Remember our mission - to protect the Zummerzet Zyder makers?"

The driver asked, "Cash, OK?"

Ella could keep quiet no longer. "No, cash is not OK. Because we don't have a recipe. We do not work for any Devon cider company. We did not bid for it. We have no interest in having a recipe. We wouldn't know what to do with it if we did! And I'm not even sure if I like cider!"

Frank stuck his face closer to the driver's window. "Did you hear my wife? No business. No bidding. No recipe. No interest. No knowledge. No sell! Satisfied?"

"Yes, for now. I believe you." The driver smiled once more, a little more sincerely this time. "However, we're not leaving Devon without Harry Sowden's recipe!"

"That's up to you. From our point of view, please just leave us alone. Stop following us. Stop scaring my wife. Just… Go away!"

"Point taken. Goodbye!" The driver wound his window up and the Land Rover chugged into life and set off towards Farringdon. Five minutes later, it came back towards them. The passenger window was wound down, "Dead end, that way. We're off back home. We need to regroup and decide upon…" he struggled to find the correct words.

"Future strategy," said the driver.

"Good. Bye!" said Frank in his best head-masterly voice!

"And good riddance," Ella whispered under her breath.

Frank and Ella got back into their car and sat there. Frank turned to Ella and saw the tears trickling down her face.

"Why don't we just go home and forget about the whole dismal business?" he said.

Ella bravely nodded.

For the next couple of days, they stayed wrapped up snugly at home. A two thousand-piece jigsaw was completed, a box set bought last year was finally viewed, and, in between, Ella caught up with her reading on her Kindle. The clouds were grey and enveloped Mutter's Moor. The rain rolled along the valley floor. There was little incentive to venture anywhere else.

As so often in Devon, on the third day, the sun shone, and Ella once more suggested a long walk to clear away the cobwebs. So, they consulted the South West Coast Path website and decided upon an eight-mile there and back walk between Colaton Raleigh and Budleigh Salterton. The walk followed the course of the River Otter as it made its gentle way to the sea.

They parked by the village hall in Church Road. Colaton Raleigh was its usual sleepy but friendly self. A few workmen were erecting scaffolding around a thatched cottage's roof preparing for it to be re-thatched. Two old ladies were discussing watercolour paintings by a front gate whilst putting up an advert for the forthcoming Colaton Raleigh Art Exhibition.

"I'm amazed there are enough artists here in Colaton Raleigh to mount an exhibition."

One of the old ladies heard him. "You'd be surprised how

creative our village can be."

"Make a note of the date," said the other, "We'll see you there."

Frank thanked them for their invitation, locked the car and, bidding the old ladies a good morning, they crossed the farm road and followed the path to the river. They turned right at the new bridge and kept the river on their left-hand side as they made their way to Otterton.

The sun rippled on the swiftly flowing river. It was higher than normal due to the recent rains. They soon passed the swing rope beloved by the children of the neighbourhood. Ella wondered how many of them actually managed to avoid a soaking in the Otter. Birds were in abundance and their song could be heard above the melodic rush of the water. Ella was on the lookout for a kingfisher, a blue bird tiny in size but always a delight to watch skimming over the river surface. Today was not a kingfisher day. Frank harboured the thought of seeing one of the otters swimming powerfully against the current. No such luck either.

However, the sky was almost Mediterranean Blue except for a few white fluffy clouds. A number of the trees were losing their leaves but still provided adequate cover and protection. It was yet another beautiful Easy Devon morning.

They reached the village of Otterton in about twenty-five minutes and decided to stop at the Mill for morning refreshment. They crossed the road bridge and made their way through the Otterton Mill car park and into the restaurant. There were a smattering of local couples and one or two from further afield if one listened to the accents emanating from the conversations. Otterton Mill was mentioned in the Domesday Book as the largest and most productive of the seventy water mills in the Otter Valley. About forty years ago, it had been restored.

"Seventy water mills in this valley!"

"Now there's just this one around here. At least, it's producing something!"

They had both seen the wholemeal flour on sale at the counter. Otterton was still a working mill.

"Where have all the others gone?" Frank asked, not expecting or needing an answer.

They found a gnarled wooden table near the stairs and sat down to people watch. Ella thought the coffee was delicious. Frank found it less so.

"A little expensive," he whispered.

"Maybe, but worth it, every once in a while."

They chatted about this and that, but Ella had something important on her mind. She spoke in an emphatic but soft voice. Frank had to lean forward to hear her.

"I miss it, Frank."

"That's a statement with a thousand answers!"

"Our detective work. I miss the information gathering, the questions to the suspects. I even miss the danger. I didn't like being as scared as I was the other day, but…"

"Nevertheless, it was exciting?"

"Yes, very much. Almost too much."

"So?"

"Let's continue. I vote we take our thoughts and evidence to WPC Knowle and see if she's got anything to add. I'm convinced more than ever that Billy's death was murder. We've got our suspects. She may have some more."

"So, who do you think did the ghastly deed?"

"I don't know. I don't think it was premeditated. I think it may have been a crime of passion. Our murderer tried to cover up their traces by muddying the waters."

"That is exactly what I have been thinking."

"You mean you been going over the motives of our suspects

as well?"

"Of course, that's why we left the whiteboard up."

"I think the girlfriend seems to be the jealous kind. Perhaps she found out about an affair?"

"True. But his ex-wife may still be in love with him? When he rejects her she takes revenge?"

"Could either of them have lifted Billy into the vat?"

"Hell hath no fury as a woman scorned."

"That's a man talking!" Ella laughed.

"William Congreve, to be exact. In 1697. He wrote a poem called The Mourning Bride. The real quote is:-

Heaven has no rage like love to hatred turned

Nor hell a fury like a woman scorned."

Ella was impressed. "And you didn't even use your phone. Sometimes you're so clever."

"English literature, O and A Level, back in the day!" Frank smiled and took a sip of coffee. It tasted much better than it did ten minutes ago.

"What about the Zummerzet Zyder Mafia?" continued Ella. "They scared me half to death but when we got to talking to them, they seemed much more timid than I imagined them to be. Except for the driver."

"Yes, he appeared to be their leader. Whenever he spoke the other two paid careful attention!"

"Perhaps they visited Billy's house," Ella continued, "Who knows what happened there? Maybe three onto one gave them boldness. It may all have got out of control very quickly."

"Yes, if they killed him in the house, they could easily have lifted him into the vat."

"It's like a symbolic ritual!"

"This is what happens if you mess about with the Zyder

Mafia!"

"Gruesome but not personal!" Ella shuddered.

"The godfather again!"

Ella had a cheeky grin on her face as she supped her coffee.

Frank continued, "Don't forget Harry Sowden. If Billy was trying to steal the recipe, who knows what might have happened. His business appeared to mean a great deal to him. Billy was stealing his cider, drip by drip. Perhaps Harry found out."

"I did enjoy his tour of the cider process. He seemed a kind, old man."

Frank disagreed. "He's younger than us. He looked strong enough to dump Billy in the barrel. But he didn't appear to be too much of a businessman."

"Gabriel Metcombe is my chief suspect at the moment. He had motive and opportunity."

"Right. And he's used to lugging beer barrels around the place." Frank pondered.

"Next steps?" Ella asked.

"Finish our walk. Let's not let this whole sordid business ruin a glorious October day!"

"Point taken, Frank. Drink up and let's head for the sea."

They continued back over the road bridge onto the riverside footpath. They followed the river and half an hour later reached South Farm Road. Here the South West Coast Path leaves the coast to go over the River Otter at its lowest crossing point. They followed the Coast Path towards the sea. It headed almost in a straight line beside the river and its salt marsh. They stopped at the bird hide alongside the path and spent ten minutes reading about the birds to be found out on the marsh. Having seen a few emigrating geese, they left the hide and carried on until they reached the Lime Kiln car park. From there, they sauntered along the seafront into Budleigh

Salterton.

The town has an unmerited reputation as God's waiting room but there were lots of people, young and old, on the promenade footpath, outside the cafes and in the beach huts.

"I like Budleigh," Frank remarked as they reached the wooden boats scattered on the stony beach.

Someone had sculpted a boat out of pebbles. A couple of walkers stopped and admired the ramshackle artwork. The town was quiet, quaint, old-fashioned, scenic, but with an atmosphere of calm dependability. Budleigh Salterton wouldn't let you down. It was a millennium away from the murder and mayhem that they had been caught up in for the past few weeks.

They loitered, sitting agreeably on one of the many wooden benches lining the path. They basked in the autumnal sunlight watching the various passers-by. Time drifted like the fallen leaves floating down the River Otter.

After a couple of hours, they realised that they had spent so much of the day in Budleigh that their legs had lost the incentive to walk the four-plus miles back to their car. Instead of retracing their steps, they wandered up the high street. Frank consulted the online bus timetable, and they caught the 157 back to Colaton Raleigh.

They enjoyed a gentle saunter down Church Road past Place Court. The old manor house was surrounded by its delightful thatched cob wall. Eventually, they arrived back at their car. The two old ladies had moved on and so did Frank and Ella back to Otterbury for a late, late afternoon tea.

"Thank you, Frank!"

"What for?"

"For a beautiful day. It did a beautiful job of clearing away the cobwebs. I'm ready to rejoin the fray. We've got a murderer to catch!"

The next day they drove into Sidmouth and walked alongside The River Sid in The Byes discussing their next steps. The River Sid is less than seven miles long yet Sidbury, Sidford and Sidmouth all received their names from its journey through their settlements. The Byes is made up of wildflower meadows and fields forming a riverside park that encourages wildlife conservation. The whole place is free for both locals and visitors to explore. Both Frank and Ella enjoyed the peaceful atmosphere. There was something restorative about the sight and sound of a river flowing through such scenic surroundings.

"We need to find what alibis our suspects have. We may be able to rule them out if their alibis stand up to scrutiny."

The Byes, as usual, was full of dog walkers and a few Lycra wearing cyclists. However, walking ahead of them on an adjacent parallel pathway was a familiar-looking purple-haired straggly woman.

"Here's our first chance to find out an alibi. It's Amelia!"

Frank and Ella quickened their pace in an attempt to question their quarry. The paths converged to make their way alongside the River Sid. Amelia slowed down and it helped Frank and Ella to draw alongside.

"Hello, Amelia!"

Amelia turned around and, as she recognised who was talking to her, she gasped.

"It's you again. What do you want?"

Frank smiled and asked in as gentle a voice as he could summon up, "Just something we were talking about earlier. You might be able to help us."

"What? I'm in a hurry!" Amelia almost snapped his head off.

"Where were you when Billy Dowd died?"

"You know. You saw me at our house."

"That was after he was already dead."

"I was in town. I had a drink at the Anchor with Agnes."

"Interesting. Billy's ex-wife?" Frank spoke quietly but with some disbelief.

"No. Agnes and I may lately have been rivals but we've been friends for a much longer time. That's how I met Billy, because of our friendship."

"Interesting."

"Stop saying that," Amelia shouted. Although Frank had deliberately kept his voice on a quiet, even keel, Amelia's voice had been getting louder and louder as the conversation continued.

Ella took a step towards Amelia, her hand out as if to comfort her.

"Get away! Leave me alone!" Amelia took a step of her own backward, without realising she was standing on the edge of the path, precariously near the riverbank. She slipped in the damp muddy grass and scrambled to regain her balance. She failed. In what seemed like super slow motion, she tumbled theatrically, arms waving and legs pumping at thin air, down into the river.

"Aargh!! Heeelp!!!"

Amelia landed with a cannonball-like splash in the River Sid. She shrieked in dismay and yapped in surprise. Momentarily, she disappeared under the water. Passers-by stopped and watched. Cyclists braked. One of them took a step towards the river as if deciding whether to dive in and rescue the submerged lady.

"Help, I can't swim!" she gurgled. Legs and arms blundered around as she sought to regain some semblance of dignity. She focused on both Frank and Ella pointing a flailing arm at them. Everyone in The Byes heard her screech, "Someone call the police! Hoodlums! Murderers. You tried to kill me!"

A helpful older lady watching the scene in distaste had already dialled 999 on her mobile phone a couple of moments earlier.

CHAPTER ELEVEN

SHE'S GONE OVER THE EDGE

The problem with troubleshooting is that trouble shoots back

The cyclist turned to his snickering partner and decided against a manly spot of rescuing. There was no need.

Amelia had managed to struggle up and was now standing wet and bedraggled in two feet of gently flowing water. The gathered crowd quickly appreciated the situation. A few giggled, smirked and laughed. Some turned away in disgust and continued their walk. One young onlooker took out his mobile phone and started taking pictures.

Amelia regained her balance and stood with both feet anchored securely to the riverbed. With a look of thunder, she then gingerly splashed her way to the riverbank and squelched her way up onto the path. Like some form of a shaggy dog, she shook from side to side as if to rid herself of the river water.

"You'll pay for this! First, you try to steal Billy, now you try to get rid of me! What next?"

Ella had spent the past few minutes trying not to laugh, but discretion eventually gave way to mirth.

"Don't be so silly. You look so comical. Drowning in two foot of water! You must admit it is funny!"

"It is not funny. I'm ...."

Amelia's reply was cut short by the sound of a police car's siren. She stared across towards Sid Park Road as the car screeched to a halt. Two officers of the law made their way to the scene of the accident.

This time there was no escape for Amelia. She stood there petrified.

WPC Knowle and PC Hydon surveyed the scene. They saw a dripping Amelia and an amused crowd.

"And what do we have 'ere, then?" PC Hydon scratched his chin.

Amelia burst into tears. "Thank heavens you're here, officers. This woman attacked me. She tried to murder me!"

"Excuse me," said Ella, "Amelia, are you crazy?"

"Calm down, please. Both of you." PC Hydon demanded in a loud voice.

"PC Hydon? Could you please ask some of these onlookers exactly what they saw?" WPC Knowle spoke into her radio. "No ambulance needed here, sir! We'll clear this up in no time!"

Amelia wheeled wetly towards the WPC. Humiliated, she was after blood, preferably Ella and Frank's.

"Did you not hear what I said? This woman attacked me. She tried to murder me. To kill me! She pushed me into the river in a fit of jealousy and revenge. She tried to drown me! You can't let her get away with it. That's twice this has happened!"

"Twice? What do you mean by twice?"

"Someone pushed me in the river a month or so ago. It might have been her in disguise!"

"Did you report it?"

"Well, no. It was much deeper, but I was just as wet though!"

PC Hydon returned. "Well, it seems as if these two were

having a bit of a barney and this one…" He pointed at Ella, "…may have pushed this one into the river!"

"That's outrageous!" shouted Ella.

PC Hydon again raised his voice, "Be quiet, please, madam. Less of the temper!"

Amelia laughed almost hysterically. Ella did not find it helpful. Every time she met Amelia, she felt threatened by the woman. Frank looked on helplessly as Ella royally lost it.

She shouted emphasising each separate word. "I have not lost my temper. I will not be quiet." She gulped in a large breath of air. The words turned into phrases. The volume was still as loud. "This woman is mad if she thinks I tried to kill her. What's more, she's just as mad if she thinks I tried to steal her boyfriend. I'm fed up with being accused by her of things I did not and could not do!"

This started Amelia off once more. "She could do it and she did do it. She tried to kill me. Ask anybody. They'll tell you the truth!"

The crowd, on the verge of dispersing, gathered once more around the action until PC Hydon took matters into his own hands.

"Right, that does it," he bellowed. "If you two do not calm down this instant, you will both be arrested for disturbing the peace!"

The threat of arrest seemed to do the trick. Ella turned to Frank and buried her face in his shoulder. Frank could feel her silently sobbing as he held her tight.

Amelia switched in an instant from the loud, insistent complainer to a shy, childlike, simpering girl. She stood there, still thoroughly soaked, like a demure miss goody two-shoes. Then she turned and squelched her way to Frank and modestly said "Sorry." He was speechless not knowing what to expect next. Amelia Nutwell simply moved past him and soggily walked away in the direction of Lymbourne Lane. The gathered crowd parted to let her go, a look of sympathy in some of their faces.

"Go home, Mr. and Mrs. Raleigh. You've provided enough entertainment for one day!"

A week later and Frank and Ella introduced their friends George and Bella to one of their favourite walks. The four of them parked their cars on the A3052 lay-by near the Bowd Inn and crossed the road by East Hill Farm near Newton Poppleford. They then climbed to the ridge of Mutters Moor and followed the level ancient tracks along to Peak Hill. They intended to drop down off Mutters Moor and make their way back home via Colaton Raleigh. It was yet another pleasant afternoon stroll.

"We should do this more often," Bella proposed as they ambled through the heathland.

The weather was warm for early November. The conversation was far removed from tales of murder and mayhem. Frank resisted the temptation to tell them about Lord Clinton or the seven separate commons.

At Peak Hill, they strolled across the field to the South West Coast Path before they turned right to head downhill in the direction of Otterton and Ladram Bay.

"Oh no, not again! She's like a ghost haunting us." Ella was staring at a purple-haired straggly figure about one hundred yards in front of them. She was heading towards them. Surely not? Another confrontation was inevitable!

"Can we hide or go some other route?"

It was too late. Amelia was too close to take avoiding action.

"Good afternoon," said Bella quietly, as they passed Amelia.

"Good aft… oh no, you two. And you've brought accomplices with you this time!"

Ella tried to ignore her.

"This is getting silly!" Frank said, "We mean you no harm. Look! No concealed weapons."

Laughing, all of them theatrically held up their hands in mock surrender. Amelia was startled and backed away, as she did a week ago in The Byes. This time, Frank saw what was about to take place a split second before it happened.

"Amelia, stop!"

Amelia took no notice and carried on backing away. She crashed into the hedge on the coastal side of the path and with a scream, disappeared from view.

Bella screamed in shock. "She's gone over the edge. It must be a two hundred foot drop to the sea!"

CHAPTER TWELVE

TROUBLE SEEMS TO BE FOLLOWING YOU AROUND

Deja Vu Again?

George's phone was out in an instant. He dialled 999. "Emergency!" he stuttered into the phone, "a woman's just gone over the edge of the cliff at Peak Hill." There was a pause. George gave his details and location to the operative on the other end of the phone.

"The police'll be here in an instant. Coastguard are on their way as well." All four stood there, immobile, stunned into silence.

"I don't believe this is happening! Not again!" murmured Ella.

It was a windless day, and they could hear the sound of the waves breaking against the beach below.

A faint cry of "Help!" broke into the silence. "Is there anybody there?"

The voice was unmistakably Amelia's and it was coming from somewhere close by yet over the cliff edge.

"Hold on," shouted Frank.

"I am, for dear life!"

"We've called the emergency services. They're on their way!"

Ella whispered, "Don't tell her the police are on their way."

"Well, at least, she can't run away this time!" Frank wryly smiled despite the situation.

Ella glanced guiltily at Frank. She didn't know what to do except stand there and wait for help.

A screeching of sirens announced the approach of a police car up Peak Hill from Sidmouth. There were no sheep in the field today, so the gate was left open. The car sped through it and bumped its way across the field towards them. It halted about 30 metres from the cliff edge. Frank and Ella's two favourite police officers jumped out.

"You again!" said PC Hydon, "What did you do this time? Push her over the cliff edge?"

"Well, not exactly push," murmured Ella.

"She's not dead. She sounds as if she's stuck some way down the cliff," said George quickly.

"WPC Knowle sprang into action. She barked the information into her phone. "Coastguard - we have a woman stuck halfway down a cliff at Peak Hill just west of Sidmouth! Yes, she's alive."

In the distance could be heard the buzz of a helicopter. It was headed towards them.

A young teenage lad came running up the coast path out of the wood from Sidmouth, "They've launched the lifeboat!"

The helicopter was almost above them.

"They had a coastguard helicopter visiting at Lympstone. That's why they're here so quickly!" WPC Knowle had to shout above the roar of the helicopter. It quickly located the onlookers.

PC Hydon called on everybody to move away from the cliff

edge and stay at least thirty metres inland. With the blast of air generated by the helicopter as it swooped over, everyone moved quickly back away from the scene. Most of them went to stand behind the police car. Cameras and smartphones started recording the proceedings with some youngsters attempting selfies with the helicopter in the background.

"I hope she's OK!" shouted Ella to Frank.

"I hope the down-blast hasn't knocked her off the cliff-face!"

"Don't even think that - let alone say it!"

One hundred feet above them, the helicopter side door slid open, and a rescuer was lowered towards the cliff. They disappeared from sight below them for a few minutes and everyone in the vicinity prayed to their gods that the coastguard would be able to do their job without a problem.

Their prayers were answered as the rescuer and Amelia were soon winched slowly back up to the helicopter. WPC Knowle and the pilot exchanged thumbs up. The helicopter closed its side door and quickly rose higher in the air before heading off towards Exeter.

A spontaneous round of applause erupted from the assembled crowd and Ella and Bella dissolved into tears. Frank and George stood there looking as if they were about to join them.

As the helicopter disappeared from sight, the crowd dispersed and went chattering on their way. PC Hydon approached the four remaining witnesses. "What happened to cause our victim to fall through a wire fence and hedge and down the cliff?"

Ella stepped forward, "It was all my fault. I raised my hands to her. She backed away and just slipped through the hedge."

WPC Knowle had heard the confession. "I think we need to get you down to the station to make a statement."

"No, please, not again. We were there for ages last time!"

"Mrs. Raleigh, are you refusing to help us?"

"Yes, I suppose I am!"

"Then you leave me with very little option. I am arresting you on suspicion of the attempted murder of Amelia Nutwell."

There was a gasp of dismay from the other three walkers. Bella burst into tears once more. George said, "But we all…"

WPC Knowle raised her hand as if she were stopping the traffic in Sidmouth High Street. "Quiet! PC Hydon, read her the caution."

WPC Knowle gently took Ella by the arm away from the cliff edge as PC Hydon spoke to Ella in a stern, official voice. "You do not have to say anything. But it may harm your defence, if you do not mention when questioned, something which you later rely on in court. Anything you do say may be given in evidence."

The policewoman took Ella off to the car and wrapped her up in a warm blanket to compensate for the shock of the situation.

Frank, George and Bella had been standing there speechless, frozen into inaction by the whole sequence of events. The reading of the police caution jolted Frank.

"Wait a minute, what are you doing? She's my wife! We were all to blame. We all raised our hands!"

"It's very sweet of you to all take the blame, Mr. Raleigh. However, we're taking your wife to the station. If you wish to help us in this matter, please meet us there!"

Frank waited at the police station for approaching half an hour before WPC Knowle appeared without Ella.

"Where's my wife?"

"Ah, my word, my apologies, I'm sorry you had to wait so long. We've been having a very interesting conversation. We were considering whether to charge Mrs. Raleigh."

"You can't do that! Where is my wife?" Frank was desperately trying to stay calm and focused. It was becoming a losing battle. "You said were considering whether to charge? Not have charged or are considering whether to charge."

"Yes, you heard me correctly."

Frank breathed an audible sigh of relief. "Does that mean...?"

"Yes, as you know, we've talked to your two friends. PC Hydon caught up with several other walkers who were in the vicinity of the incident. They all agreed that the raising of the hands was in 'mock surrender'. A silly thing to do but not an action that could be deemed attempted murder."

"Can I see my wife? Where is she?"

"She's in our interview room and, yes, I'd like you to join us. I thought you might like to know a little bit more about Billy Bowd."

Frank followed WPC Knowle. He was soon sat down beside his wife with a cup of tea in one hand and both his wife's hands in the other.

Frank jumped in before WPC Knowle could utter a word. "Yes, I know what you're going to say. We have not exactly kept to your request to leave it all alone. We've been to talk with all our suspects and now we're checking their alibis."

"Interesting. And who are your suspects?"

"Amelia and Agnes, obviously. They always say to look at the nearest and dearest first of all. They were both pretty jealous of anyone who came near Billy. Perhaps one of them got fed up with his philandering ways."

"I agree. Who else?"

"Harry Sowden, Billy's boss at Sowden Valley Cider Farm. Billy may have been trying to blackmail him. Harry seems like a decent bloke, but appearances can be deceptive."

Ella had been on the verge of joining in the conversation and she now added, "The Zummerzet Zyder Mafia."

Frank agreed, "Yes, they desperately want to get the recipe of the cider. But they appear to me to be comic book characters with their sunglasses and sharp suits! Again, appearances could be deceptive."

WPC Knowle smiled. "You mean, like you and Ella?"

"Yes, good point. Do we need an alibi as well?"

"Probably. Who else?"

Ella gasped and fell silent.

Frank continued. "Gabriel Metcombe, the publican of the Mariners next door to Billy. He's been getting Sowden Valley cider on the cheap. In fact, Billy drowned in cider from the farm."

"No, he didn't."

"Yes, he.... Oh, I see what you mean. Have you been doing some investigating of your own?"

"Yes, but just our normal procedures in the event of death by a person or persons unknown. He didn't drown. He was already dead when he was dumped in the cider vat."

Ella again jumped in, "He either hit his head on the stone fireplace or was hit with some object in the front room. There were blood spots on the carpet!"

WPC Knowle nodded, "You were right to deduce that some altercation, some lively discussion, had been taking place. There was a broken vase dumped in the dustbin."

"With fingerprints?"

"Unfortunately, not. Somebody either wiped their fingerprints off any surfaces, or they were wearing gloves."

"But it looks as if it could be murder?" asked Frank.

"Yes, it might be."

"Despite PC Hydon's confident comment that no one gets murdered in Sidmouth?" Ella couldn't resist that comment!

"Yes, in spite of my colleague's rather frivolous comment."

"So, you are investigating further?"

"Yes, CID are up to their necks in that serial killer case in Exeter. They've asked us to gather information until they're ready to take over."

"Us, do you mean Ella and me as well?"

WPC Knowle laughed "No, certainly not. You are both to stay well out of it. The murderer may strike again and now, either of you may be a target, if they see you nosing about."

"Please, could you tell us about when he died?"

"Oh no, you tell me what you were doing that day. If I find your alibi checks out, then I'll let you know some more information."

Frank told her about the morning walk with their friends George and Bella.

"They were the people you were with this afternoon up at Peak Hill? The ones I've just been talking to?"

"Yes, they'll vouch for us!"

"They already have!"

Frank continued to relate the telephone conversation with the post office at lunchtime. Ella reminded him about the drive to deliver the package, the car park ticket and what they found when they arrived at the house.

"Right, I'll need to check the telephone call, with your permission, of course. I've already seen and dealt with the parking ticket."

"You'll find all the things we've told you are the absolute truth."

"Good. Now there is one thing that puzzles me."

Frank looked puzzled. "Only one thing? What?"

"The package. We forgot all about it. I went back this morning and couldn't find it. What was in it? Where did you leave it? I think you and Ella need to meet me tomorrow morning at the house and show me exactly where you left it."

"Are we free to go now?"

"Yes, trouble seems to be following you around. I hope your alibis do check out. We will not be charging Mrs. Raleigh for this afternoon's almost tragic accident."

Ella looked relieved and ready to burst into tears. She gripped Frank's hand even tighter.

"I think you're a lovely couple but if I find out you are murderers then heaven help you both. Now, go home!"

The next morning, WPC Knowle phoned Ella and Frank to tell them that their alibis had both panned out.

Frank had no doubt they would. She continued by asking both of them if they could meet her at Twenty three, River Street in Sidmouth at around about eleven o'clock?

"We'll be there," responded Ella.

"Eleven on the dot," said Frank.

WPC Knowle was waiting at the gate of Billy's house at the appointed hour. Frank and Ella walked with her to the front door. Frank reached down to get the key from under the right-hand flowerpot. It wasn't there.

"Did any of the police team remove the key from under this flowerpot?"

"No, why?"

"It's gone, have you got it?"

"No, we put it back there when we'd finished all our investigations. We always try to put things back as we found them. I assumed Amelia or Agnes would use it."

"Maybe."

Ella had an idea. "Frank, there are two flowerpots, one on each side. The police probably replaced it under the other flowerpot. They weren't to know which one you found it under!"

WPC Knowle nodded in agreement. "Check the other one!"

Frank knelt down once more and reached under the left-hand flowerpot.

"Very strange. It's not there either! Someone has taken it."

CHAPTER THIRTEEN

DRINK UP, FRANK

You're never too old to learn something stupid.

Frank and Ella stood there not quite knowing what to do next.

WPC Knowle looked at them both before smiling, "Do you think I'd have come here without a key?"

Husband and wife stood there in silent appreciation.

"I spoke to Amelia just after Billy's death and asked her if I could have a copy of the front door key just in case we needed it. We got a copy made and it's been included in the case files. I picked it up this morning before I came here. In any case, how do you think I got in the other day?"

Ella spoke up, "I don't think we thought that one through!"

"No, now let's get inside and see if there's anything in that package that will be helpful."

"I left it on the table behind the front door," said Frank with confidence.

WPC Knowle unlocked the door and immediately peered behind the door. "There's a table here, but no package."

Frank and Ella didn't need to confirm her statement, but they did all the same. No, the tabletop was empty. There was no package on, beside or under the table.

Ella stopped and put her finger to her lips. "Ssssh, listen."

Frank and WPC Knowle stood stock still for about fifteen seconds. They heard no sounds within the house.

"Sorry," said Ella, "I thought I heard someone in the kitchen. Must have been something outside on the road."

They walked through to the kitchen only to find it empty. The back door was closed, and the courtyard was also empty.

For forty minutes they searched everywhere. Indoors up and downstairs. Throughout all the house. They went out into the courtyard. There was no package. Frank investigated behind the now empty Cider Vat and found a small wooden gate that blended into the surrounding fence.

"That's how she disappeared on that day," murmured Frank.

"Pardon?" replied the nearby Ella.

"When Amelia vanished into thin air on the day of the murder, she simply went through this gate."

Ella jumped in. "That's how she escaped. As it's behind the Cider Vat we couldn't and didn't want to explore around here."

"Look, it doesn't fit perfectly." Frank examined the handle. "The catch is broken. Anyone could push it open from either side."

WPC Knowle had overheard the brief conversation. "The gate leads on to the alleyway between the pub and this house. Anyone from the pub could have got into this courtyard through the gate."

"But they couldn't get into the house. Both front and back doors are undamaged," Frank stated.

"We opened the back door from the inside quite easily but there's no way you can get in without a key." The policewoman wrote down the information in her black notebook.

"So," Ella added, "whoever killed Billy had to have a key to get into the house."

"Or," WPC Knowle concluded, "Billy knew his killer!"

They all retreated indoors as the first spots of a November rain shower quickly dotted the paving stones in the courtyard.

"I said I'd share some information with you after I'd checked your alibis!" WPC Knowle consulted her black notebook. "I interviewed all your suspects about their whereabouts on the day of Billy's death."

Ella and Frank sat up and paid attention.

"I asked Amelia where she was. She says she was in Seaton with Agnes. The hourly bus from Seaton gets into Sidmouth at a quarter to the hour. So they both could have been in Sidmouth when he was killed."

"Harry told us he was in Barnstaple at the Pannier Market," Frank added.

"Strange, he told me he was in Tiverton at their market."

WPC Knowle continued. "Two of the Zummerzet Zyder Mafia were away in Jersey at a Cider Festival on the day of Billy's death. Can't really be in two places at once!"

"I'd love to know what was in that package and why it's gone missing," said Ella.

"There definitely was a package?"

"Absolutely definitely", replied Ella.

"Well, it's not here. I'll put in a report about our search. I don't think, there's anything more we can do here."

Frank asked WPC Knowle, "Can we leave by the gate in the courtyard? Just to see how it's done and where it leads."

WPC Knowle nodded. The rain shower had already passed over. Frank and Ella rapidly crossed the courtyard, opened the wooden gateway and stepped into the alley. Within fifteen seconds, they had reached the entrance to the saloon bar of the Mariners pub.

Frank was following Ella in when she came to an abrupt

standstill. He bumped into her almost knocking both of them onto the floor. Ella raised a finger to her lips telling him to be silent before she hastily retreated back to the alleyway.

"What was that all about?" asked Frank.

Ella was not happy. "In there I saw three gentlemen of distinctly different heights talking with the landlord."

"The Zummerzet Zyder Mafia? They were there last time."

"The very ones." Ella's face was rapidly losing its colour. "I'm not going in the Mariners to face them again. They scare me. I've had enough scares recently to last a lifetime - a very long lifetime!"

Frank stood still for a while. His furrowed brow suggested he was thinking deeply.

"Right. Here's the plan. You ensconce to The Dairy Shop in Church Street. Buy as many coffees as you like. I'll wait here and see what's happens. I'll either talk to Gabriel when they've gone or follow them for a while. I'll see if any of them has an alibi for the day of the murder."

"Are you sure?"

"I can't think of a better plan. We wanted to confirm all of our suspects' alibis. They may tell us a different story than they told WPC Knowle. Just like Harry did. Here's my chance to get two more for the price of one!"

"OK but be safe. I didn't move down here to end up on my own!"

"I'll be as safe as the Bank of England!"

"I've got my phone with me. Phone me with an update."

"Will do. See you in a short while!"

Ella moved quickly along the alleyway out into River Street and disappeared from view.

Frank took a deep breath and went back into The Mariners.

The Zummerzet Zyder Mafia were still there. They looked as if they were earnestly engaged in conversation with Gabriel Metcombe. Gabriel rose to his feet when Frank entered the saloon bar.

"Good affnoon, sir. Pleased to see 'ee again. What can I get 'ee?"

Gabriel's Devonian accent was very pronounced. He had turned away from the mafia towards Frank with a look of relief.

"Hello, landlord. The last time I was in here you barred me!"

"Yes, but I'm willing to let bygones be bygones. Now, do 'ee wanna drink?"

"Yes, but," Frank decided to play a little game, "please serve these gentlemen first." He then put on as good a piece of ham acting as he could manage. His voice tone changed to one of complete surprise. "Oh, my goodness me, it's you three."

"You know each other?" Gabriel was confused.

"Well, not exactly. We have bumped into each other before. But we've never been properly introduced."

"That's easily remedied." The tallest gentlemen stepped forward. He had been the front seat passenger in the Land Rover. He removed his sunglasses and extended his right hand. Frank and he exchanged a handshake.

"My name's Frank Raleigh, but you probably already know that."

"We've seen you around. My name is Norbert Fitzwarren. I hail from the ancient county town of Taunton from the famous county of Somerset, home of Taunton Norton, the best cider in the whole wide world!"

"I'm sure some would dispute that claim." Frank smiled.

"But my name is Norbert Fitzwarren. Why would I lie?"

"No, that's not what I meant. Oh, never mind!"

The shortest of the two remaining gentlemen also stepped forward, removing his sunglasses and raising his right hand. Frank once again shook the proffered hand.

"And my name is Delbert Fitzpaine. I also hail from the famous cider country of Somerset."

"Ah yes," said Frank, "You're the joker of the pack. The one with all the silly death jokes."

"How do you know?" Delbert appeared completely surprised.

"My wife and I were in the Mustard Seed Café one day when you walked in. You were waiting for a funeral to finish before going off to meet our landlord!"

"You're well informed and very observant," said Norbert with a twisted smile.

"Yes, I suppose I am. Pleased to meet you both. And you…"

This time Frank extended his right hand and shook the hand of the driver of the Land Rover.

The man kept his sunglasses on and, in a quiet, gentle voice explained, "My name is Albert Fitzhead."

"Now that we know each other, let me buy you all a drink. Landlord, four pints of your finest cider."

All three gentlemen at once shook their heads and raised their hands in protest. "No, no, no!"

"Sorry, did I say something wrong?"

"Not at all," replied Norbert, "it's just that none of us actually drink cider. We hate the taste of it. Give us a glass of good old fashioned orange juice any day."

"All right, OK. Well, three pints…"

"Half pints," interrupted Norbert the tall one.

Three half-pints of your finest orange juice, please, landlord!"

Drinks were served and the four moved over to a table by the window. Frank played the role of interrogator knowing he had nothing to lose.

"Why are you here in The Mariners if you don't drink? It can't be the company, there's hardly anybody else here."

Delbert answered, "We are the salesmen for Taunton Norton Cider. The company has been brewing cider since 1805. We tour suitable public houses in the South West. We allow these establishments to sell our cider."

"Naturally, we give them the best deals possible. It is a cut-throat business. Margins are tight."

Norbert added, "This month it is Sidmouth's turn to benefit from our refreshing drink."

Albert joined in. "Gabriel's just about to agree a very beneficial deal... for him."

Gabriel, who had been rather obviously listening in to the conversation, shook his head in disagreement.

Norbert continued, "Drink up. We're doing the rounds this afternoon. There are several public houses here in Sidmouth who would benefit from selling Taunton Norton."

Frank decided to play along. "Can we all fit in your Land Rover?"

Norbert shook his head. "No, we left that back in Taunton. No, we're in the Kia Sorento today. A most agreeably large car with which to impress the locals!"

"Except," Delbert added, "we won't need the car this afternoon. All the public houses are well within walking distance."

Before they left the Mariners, Frank decided to probe them about an alibi. "I've been reading about cider production. Have you heard of La Fais'sie d'Cidre?"

Tall Norbert smiled. "Heard about it? We were there - all three of us. Just about a month or so ago. Flew over from Bristol."

"It was a wonderful time. Jersey at this time of year is still a very acceptable place to visit. We all enjoyed our time on the island. We were successful in creating a number of links that will increase our slender profit margins greatly in the foreseeable future."

"That's interesting!"

Short Delbert chipped in. "Yes, take a look on my phone. I've got loads of pictures of the festival." He shoved the phone in front of Frank's face. "That's Hamptonne Country Life Museum where it all took place. Beautiful grounds. Lots of people. Lots of drink. Although we just stuck to the bottled water."

"And orange juice, of course," said Norbert.

Frank finished his pint of cider and accepted the invitation to join them on their pub sales crawl. He phoned Ella and told her to go home, and he'd phone her when he'd finished. Reluctantly, Ella agreed. "Take care of yourself."

Four pubs later, Frank had found no further incriminating evidence about the Mafia. He had however enjoyed their sales pitch, their enthusiasm for their products and their generosity. They bought him a pint of cider at each pub. "Drink up, Frank!"

Frank was not a big drinker but his upbringing dictated that he could not be rude to his companions. He emptied his glass. Although he was drinking Devon Cider none of the three gentlemen commented upon this choice of beverage.

Their generosity and affability towards Frank was not reciprocated by the landlords in each of the four pubs they visited. Each one was fiercely protective of their Devon heritage. Their loyalty was to St Petroc's flag. Taunton Norton would not appear on the list of ciders for sale.

The Zummerzet Zyder Mafia were getting used to this partisan Devonian behaviour so they turned their attention to making sure Frank had an afternoon to remember… or was an afternoon to forget? Bit by bit, Frank became a little less in control as the afternoon wore on. His speech became a little more slurred. His hands were a little more unsteady.

"I'm not used to this ci-i-i-der. Stoo mud. I need some faresh hair."

Norbert and Delbert waved goodbye to him outside the last of the pubs.

Albert stood beside him and conveyed a parting message to him in a calm mannered voice, "Nice to meet you, Mr. Raleigh. Pity you didn't seem to think our offer for the recipe was acceptable. Go home carefully."

"Ai'll fone Hella from the seafront."

He weaved his uncertain way towards the seafront. He made slow and unsteady progress. It took him ten minutes to reach the end of York Street. Stepping off the pavement to cross the road junction, he never saw the Kia Sorento coming around the corner.

CHAPTER FOURTEEN

LAMBS IN WOLVES' CLOTHING?

Wives sometimes make fools of their husbands, but most husbands are the do-it-yourself type.

An old lady, calling her cat in for its evening meal, shouted "Watch out, young man!"

Her cat dashed across the road. The Sorento braked and veered away from Frank giving him the time, even in his befuddled state, to step back away from the middle of the road. He tripped on the kerb and came to a rest on his hands and knees on the narrow pavement.

The Sorento narrowly missed him, Albert waving condescendingly from the driver's seat as he drove on without stopping.

Frank sat down on the kerb, heads in his hands, tears rolling down his face. He was suddenly, unaccountably sober.

A concerned teenager leaned over him whilst also holding the old lady's cat. The cat was purring contentedly, "Hey mister, are you alright?"

"Not really."

"Diddy. Diddy. You almost got run over by that nasty big car." The teenager stroked Diddy before handing the cat back to its owner. He then turned back to Frank.

"Mister, you don't look at all well. Can I phone anyone for you? Can I get you a Taxi? You can't drive home in your condition."

"Yes, please. Taxi."

The teenager took out his phone and within five minutes a taxi had arrived. Frank remembered where he lived. As he poured himself into the taxi, he turned to the boy. "Thank you. S'good to know there's youngsters as kind as you in Sidmouth. What's yer name?"

"George. And this is my dad Rupert. He owns the taxi company."

"Thank you once again. My wife is going to kill me."

"Best let Dad explain when he gets you home."

When Frank arrived home, Ella was not there. He thanked the taxi driver once again, let himself in and tottered sheepishly off to sleep in the spare room. As he lay there dozing, he questioned where Ella might be. He spent five minutes trying to check his phone before finding a message from her. She said she had met an old friend and would be back in an hour or two.

Ella was almost telling Frank the truth. Billy's ex-wife, Agnes was someone's old friend, just not an old friend of Ella.

Ella ventured into The Dairy Shop to find herself sitting at an adjoining table to Agnes. She smiled humbly only to be invited by Agnes to sit at her table. Despite previous disagreements, Ella moved her coffee across to the table and sat down. Agnes' eyes looked as if they were waving a white flag of truce. They both started talking in a somewhat civilised manner.

"They've kept her in hospital for a couple of days. They're very worried about her." Agnes' face relaxed. She appeared relieved to be able to unburden herself.

Ella lowered her voice so as not to inform the whole shop about their conversation. "Why are they worried?"

Agnes' voice also quietened in mutual co-operation.

"They think she's had a bit of a breakdown. After Billy died, it's been one thing after another. You know about the river dunking and the cliff rescue."

"Yes, she seemed close to the edge of sanity. The cliff must have tipped her over!"

"Exactly. Well, she'd slept for one night in the River Street house but then refused to go back again. She could have done so at any time. It'll be her house. I don't mind. I made sure he kept up his life insurance payments!"

"Did she have her own key?"

"Of course. Billy made sure she could come and go as she pleased. She's got one and I've still got mine."

"Did she have a house of her own?"

"No, she was in a rented flat. She met up with Billy and spent so much time there that she gave up the flat."

"What about her belongings?"

She's got clothes and stuff there. Amelia was never a materialistic girl. Just the basic essentials. Mostly purple."

Ella and Agnes sipped at their coffees.

"She did go back once to pick some of those things up." Agnes stared out of the window at the people meandering along Church Street.

"Will she stay with you or live in Billy's house when they let her out of the hospital?" Ella was happy to ask the nonthreatening questions.

"No, she'll be staying with two of my friends up in Woolbrook. One's a nurse and the other was once a doctor. It seemed the best place for her."

Ella emptied her cup and offered to buy a second cup and a slice of cake for both of them. There was a companionable silence until the coffee and cake appeared on their table.

"He wasn't such a bad sort, I suppose." Agnes reminisced.

"Who?"

"Billy. I've known far worse. However, I've known far better."

"Such a strange way to die."

"Yes, had it happened up at his workplace, I would have laughed and thought it apt. Even typical. You read about workers drowning after falling into vats or containers."

Ella ventured forth into alien territory and told Agnes how Frank and herself had discovered Billy. She didn't say why they were there at the house. "We found the door wide open and went in to tell the owners. What a day that was. I'll never forget it!"

"Absolutely. Amelia and I travelled over by bus to Seaton to look in a few second-hand shops. I buy stuff at boot fairs and second-hand places and then sell them on eBay and the like."

"Were you there all day?"

"No, just the morning and then we came back to Sidmouth for some lunch."

"What time did you get back from Seaton?"

"The bus dropped us off just before noon. We split up very briefly and wandered through some of the second-hand shops down the High Street. But we were here in The Dairy Shop for lunch at about 12.30. We stayed gossiping and arguing for a couple of hours. In fact, John behind the counter asked us to leave because we were getting a little loud…"

"A little loud?"

"To be honest, we were shouting at each other." Agnes laughed in embarrassment.

"What about?"

"I've no idea. We can be best buddies one minute and the worst of enemies a minute later."

"I noticed Amelia appeared to have a bit of a temper."

"Yes, we both have," Agnes smiled warmly, "But our anger dies down as soon as one of us smiles or cracks a silly comment."

"Lambs in wolves' clothing?"

"That's us! Amelia then went back to Billy's."

"Yes, we know!"

"Of course, you do. I went back in here, apologised profusely to John, bought a pot of tea and a cream cake and stayed here for most of the afternoon. I checked a couple of possibilities on eBay and then went back to my flat near the cricket ground."

The conversation meandered onto other matters. Ella was intrigued about how Agnes could make money on eBay. Agnes launched into a detailed explanation of her buying and selling strategy. Time flew by.

Ella wanted to find out one more thing. She couldn't think of a way to casually introduce it so she decided to just blurt it out and hope for the best.

"When Frank went upstairs to check whether there was anyone in the house, he found a strange sight on the bedroom floor."

Agnes laughed a little too loudly again. She knew what was coming. "Billy's best shirt and trousers. He only had one pair that were best. He only wore them on special occasions. The day before he died, I must admit, I went to the house."

"What did you do?"

"What do you think? I cut them up with a pair of pinking shears."

"Pinking shears?"

"Yes, I use them in my dressmaking."

But why are they called pinking shears?"

"I thought about that a while ago. I did some research. It's because they produce an edge similar to the petal edges of a pink carnation."

"I never knew that!" Ella grinned and beamed.

"The shears leave a lovely zigzag pattern instead of a straight cut. They slow down the rate of fray."

"On the edges of the cloth?"

"Exactly!"

"Any symbolic reason for using them?"

"No. They cut cloth better than any other of my other scissors!"

It was nearing closing time.

Ella checked her watch. "Oh, look at the time. I really need to be going."

"Same here. It was good to talk. I feel much better than I did this morning."

"Frank thought that someone had broken into the house and vandalised it!"

"No, it was me. I confess."

"You broke into the house?"

"No, don't be silly. Why would I need to break in when both Amelia and I have our own keys?"

Ella bade Agnes a fond farewell as she walked back to the car before driving home.

Ella arrived home to discover Frank snoring away in the spare bedroom. He smelled distinctly of cider. Ella decided not to wake him and would wait for a convincing explanation in the morning.

CHAPTER FIFTEEN

A COMPLETE SET OF ALIBIS

Life begins at the end of your comfort zone.

There was an uneasy silence in the Raleigh household the next morning. Frank had a hangover – his first for very many years. Ella had learned from decades of married experience to wait for the whole story before exploding.

A late breakfast had finished before either said a word.

"Sorry." Frank said with genuine remorse, "They played me like a mug!"

"A cider mug?"

"You recognised the smell?"

"Couldn't avoid it. I decided to leave you to sleep it off in the spare room."

More silence.

"Who's they?"

"The Zummerzet Zyder Mafia!"

"Tell me the whole story. It could be important!"

"From what I can remember, they were in Sidmouth to sell Taunton Norton…"

Ella raised an eyebrow.

"It's their brand of cider. They were trying to get the

Sidmouth pubs to stock it. However, despite various incentives, none of them would. All the pubs we visited stayed loyal to the Devon ciders that they already stock."

Ella's anger had toned down to annoyance.

"Is that all?"

"No, after the fourth pub, they said they'd finished. They were fed up with being refused by all the pubs. I think they got me drunk to teach me not to interfere."

"Probably!"

"Well, then they left me and I was going to walk to the seafront for some fresh air and then phone you. As I was crossing York Street - rather unsteadily, mind - a Kia Sorento nearly knocked me over."

"My word, were you injured?"

"No, only my pride. The car came closer to killing an old lady's cat than me."

"Yes, but cats have got nine lives. You've only got one!"

"The worst of it was that the driver smiled at me as he passed by."

"Why would anyone do that?"

"I don't know why. I do know who."

Ella raised her eyebrows. "Who?"

"Albert, the middleman in the Zummerzet Zyder Mafia."

Ella hugged Frank to her as tightly as he could ever remember. For several minutes they stayed like that in the middle of the room. Eventually, to Frank's disappointment, Ella released him and asked, in a soft voice "What about their alibi?"

"It's a good one. They were all in Jersey at the time of the murder for a Cider Festival. How do we check out their alibi?"

"Wait a minute. Didn't WPC Knowle say only two of them went? The other could have bumped Billy off."

"Are you sure? I missed that."

"She definitely said two. She must have known there are three of them."

"We're going to have to chat to WPC Knowle."

"Why?" although as she asked, she knew the reason why. "Because she'll be able to confirm or deny their alibi. She can check with the airline and the Cider Festival organisers. She can find out how many of them went to Jersey."

"Exactly. Now, what about you?"

"Yesterday. Did you have a good chat with your friend?"

"Very interesting."

"Was it Bella?"

"No. Agnes!"

"Billy's ex-wife?" Frank regretted even slightly raising his voice.

"The very one! I've gathered two more alibis. Agnes and Amelia were in Seaton all morning shopping in second-hand stores."

"How did they get…?"

"There and back by bus. They were in The Dairy Shop for lunch and for most of the afternoon."

"John behind the counter confirmed it."

"So, when Billy was being killed, they were either in Seaton, on a bus or in the Dairy Shop."

"Looks that way."

Frank's head gradually returned to normal. During the afternoon he could be seen standing in front of the whiteboard busily scribbling away. The alibi column was looking full, almost crowded.

"So we've got alibis for Agnes, Amelia, Harry and the Zummerzet Zyder mafia."

Ella raised herself out from her armchair and stood beside her husband.

"The only one without an alibi is Gabriel Metcombe, our friendly landlord at the Mariners. We need to speak to him."

"I don't want to go near another pub for quite a while yet."

"You have no choice. I'm not going there alone!"

"Yes, you're right."

"Ella expects every man to do his duty!"

"Thank you, admiral."

"I think you've learned your lesson."

"Indeed, I'm sticking to the orange and lemonade from now on!"

"Let's get going. The sooner we hear his excuse, the sooner we can meet WPC Knowle and then the sooner we catch our murderer."

Before they entered the pub, they checked their phone apps were recording. Uncharged phones were a thing of the past in the Raleigh household.

Quicker than Frank would have wanted, he found himself alongside Ella in the saloon bar of the Mariners. A few locals were enjoying a lunchtime drink. Gabriel recognised them immediately. "Welcome, quite the locals, bain't 'ee?"

"We're not here to drink," said Ella.

"I thought that was the whole point of a pub like this?"

"No, it's a social hub of the community as well," replied Frank, a little too smugly.

"And we're on a social visit," added Ella.

"Social, is it? Well, let's hear your sparkling conversation."

Frank jumped straight in, eager to be off the premises sooner rather than later.

"Where were you on the day of the murder of Billy Bowd?"

"Now, there's a leading question. You're asking a man who has a legitimate claim to be Billy's killer where he was. On the day of his murder?"

"That was the question. Have you got an answer?"

"Yes. It's the same as I told the policewoman. I was here, behind this bar, with about fifteen witnesses."

A couple of the other people in the saloon bar, sitting and standing close by, nodded their heads in agreement.

"I just finished a meeting with the manager of Billy's cider. It could have been a bit embarrassing. I hoped he didn't want to drink any of the cider, seeing as 'ee made it in the first place!"

Frank and Ella had their complete set of alibis. There was no satisfaction in achieving their target.

"One other thing. Have you got a key to Billy's house?"

"Let me think. You asking that question has triggered some sort of memory. Yes, as a matter of fact, I do have a key. I remember now. He gave me one a couple of years ago when I was having some redecoration work done upstairs. I stayed in his spare bedroom for a couple of nights. I just never gave it back to him."

Ella smiled at him and said "Thank you for answering our questions. Good afternoon!"

She turned and headed for the door closely followed by Frank. Both Frank and Ella prayed their phone apps were still working.

"A complete set of alibis!"

"Now for WPC Knowle."

A phone-call to the police station told them that WPC Knowle was out on patrol and would contact them if they left a phone number. Frank and Ella went home and checked their recordings. Frank had transferred all their recordings onto the computer, converted them to mp3 files and then burned them onto a CD for safekeeping.

The next evening WPC Knowle, Frank and Ella sat down in the interview room of the police station to compare notes. Both Frank and Ella saw no reason to hold back any information. They shared the suspect's motives and alibis and their own recordings. "I'm sure this is inadmissible evidence," said WPC Knowle with a smile on her face.

A full discussion followed.

"This package still concerns me. No-one knew about it except the sender. That sender could have been Billy or Harry or the Mafia or anyone."

"But if they sent it, why try to get it back?"

"What if Billy sent it and someone else wanted it back?"

"Why would he send it to himself?"

"Because that might be the only way to smuggle it out. Perhaps he volunteered to take the post to a post box. I don't know."

"There was no sign of a break-in but….."

"My gut instinct says it must be still there, somewhere." WPC Knowle was well known in the East Devon division for her hunches or feminine intuitions.

"Let's go back and search again," said Ella.

"Can't do any harm?"

They agreed to meet the next morning.

"Same time, same place?"

"Eleven o'clock on the dot!"

WPC Knowle brought the key from the case files. Frank, for old times sake, couldn't help but check under the flowerpots for the key he originally found on that fateful October day.

"I don't believe it!"

He stood there holding up a key in his left hand. He tried it in the door which smoothly opened.

Ella was puzzled. "It wasn't there the last time we looked."

"Someone must have put it back." WPC Knowle was already jotting that fact in her black notebook.

"I thought I heard someone in the house when we first arrived the last time."

"Maybe, but how did they get out? We were standing by the front door for quite some time."

"It's obvious," Ella said in a smug whisper, "through the gate. It was easy to open. Frank said that the latch was broken."

"I wonder," interrupted Frank, "if the package is in the cider vat?"

"Why do you think that?"

"Well, if the person you may have heard was after the package, then they had to have escaped through the back courtyard and through the gate."

"Yes, that makes a peculiar sort of sense," added Ella.

"But," said WPC Knowle, "if someone was here, if someone used that key to get in, wouldn't they have just taken the whole package with them? Why leave the package behind?"

"Perhaps they panicked? Perhaps, oh I don't know!" Frank shrugged his shoulders.

"Well, the only place we didn't search was inside the Cider

Vat. It had been emptied after Billy's death so we just assumed no one would bother with it."

"There's only one way to prove or disprove your theory."

They went through the house and into the courtyard.

Ella approached the huge Vat. "The lid's been left half off, half on."

"Perhaps they were hoping to let the smell waft away on the breeze."

"I bet there's some rain gathered in it. Be careful."

WPC Knowle had grabbed a chair from the kitchen. She placed it by the vat and was standing on it.

"What can you see?"

"It's dark but I think you may be correct."

"How did you know?" Ella was impressed.

"You've got feminine intuition. Us men, we just get lucky!"

WPC Knowle was balanced precariously over the edge of the vat, "I can't reach it. It looks like some sort of parcel."

"We need a plan of action." Ella said, "Come down. Let's think!"

They all went into the kitchen and stood facing the vat, hands metaphorically stroking their chins.

"There's enough room to tip the Vat over on its side."

"It might roll around a bit."

"What about those implements gardeners use to trim branches above their reach?"

"A tree pruner?"

"We might cut the package in half if we apply too much force!"

"One of us lift up the package using the pruner and then reach in and grab it."

"We could use those things they use in the Byes to pick up

litter."

"We need a contraption that they used to have in the amusement arcades on the pier. A sort of Meccano crane."

"I think we're getting into the realms of fantasy now!"

"Agreed!"

"I think our best bet is to tip it over."

The three of them worked out where they wanted the Cider Vat to fall over and how they should apply the lifting pressure. Frank and WPC Knowle heaved the lid off and left it leaning up against the fence out of harm's way. Ella found several stones and bricks around the garden.

"We put the stones on each side of the Vat to wedge it in place."

"Good idea. Now, everyone in position," commanded WPC Knowle. They lifted, strained and heaved but achieved absolutely nothing.

"We need more oomph!"

"PC Hydon?" Ella suggested.

"That'll do it!" WPC Knowle took out her radio and summoned help from her taller, broader colleague.

Fifteen minutes later the four of them were assembled. Roles were allocated, positions taken and weight applied. Success! The vat toppled over. Three of them manhandled the wooden monstrosity whilst Ella wedged the bricks and stones into position underneath the vat where it met the gravel and paving.

"Gert, good job!" PC Hydon gave his honest Devonian opinion.

Frank took a look inside. He lay down on the ground and crawled into the heart of the beast before bringing out an object.

"That's the package!" shouted Ella.

"It definitely is the package. One problem though, it's empty." Frank found the open end of the package, turned it upside down and gave it a shake. A fair number of drops of water dripped out but nothing else. "Someone's been here before us."

"'Ello, be that the Sidmouth 'erald? Good. I've got 'ee a stary. A stary fer your nooospaper. There be an empty cider vat 'olding an empty package. It's all part of a murder scene. In Sidmouth. Murders don't 'appen in Sidmouth, do ey? Oi'm a nony mouse, a concerned reader. I'll 'ave more zoon. Cheers."

"Aretha, there's some bloke on the phone again. Talking about a cider vat. Didn't we have a phone call like that a while back?"

"Yeah, the drunkard again. There's no story in a drunkard's ramblings. We've got more important things to cover. There's a town council committee meeting. They're discussing the allotments budget tonight."

CHAPTER SIXTEEN

WHY DON'T 'EE DO A PIERROT?

I don't have a solution, but I do admire the problem.

"What do we do now?" Ella was disappointed.

"What were 'ee specting to find in there?" PC Hydon was interested to hear their ideas. They were all seated around the kitchen table.

"I was certain we were going to find some evidence that would pin the crime on one of our suspects."

"Yes, but what were 'ee specting to find?"

Frank took up the challenge. "Well, it depends on who was the murderer."

"If it was Agnes or Amelia, I'm sure we'd find a threatening letter with some evidence of his wayward manner."

WPC Knowle was scribbling notes down as far as she was able.

"If it was Harry, then some sort of proof that Billy was blackmailing him. Perhaps he was trying to blackmail him back?"

"Perhaps," WPC Knowle began, putting her pen down for a moment, "if it was the Zummerzet Zyder Mafia, proof about bribing him to provide them with the recipe?"

"Could be." Frank continued, "If it was Gabriel, then evidence about the illicit cider!"

"I don't think we'll ever know now," sighed Ella.

"This case is getting to be complicated. Everybody has a motive and everybody has an alibi," WPC Knowle summed up.

PC Hydon broke the silence. "Why don't 'ee do a Pierrot?"

"I don't understand? Do some type of continental clown?" Ella's eyebrows were raised.

"No, no, Pierrot, that chap on the TV with the moustache and the funny walk." PC Hydon persisted.

"Ah, you mean Poirot, Hercule Poirot, the famous Belgian detective!"

"That's the man!" PC Hydon clapped his hands in delight. " 'Ee gathers all the suspects together in the ole library. 'Ee runs through all the clues, all their alibis and motives. Then 'ee uses his little grey cells to reveal who killed the Colonel in the Study with the candlestick."

"I get your point, but I prefer Murder in Paradise."

PC Hydon turned to Ella. "What's Murder in Paradise and what do they do?"

She explained. "It's a TV show. It's got a formula. In each episode, the police detective gathers everybody together in a room and goes through the evidence before confronting the villain. They usually confess before they're taking away in handcuffs by the other police officers there."

PC Hydon interrupted. "It's just like I said - doing a Poirot."

"Yes, but we like Murder in Paradise. It's much better than Poirot."

"Yes," added WPC Knowle, "I don't like Poirot as much as Miss Marple. She's so good at listening and then using her life experience to work out a solution."

Everyone in the kitchen nodded in agreement. WPC Knowle

leaned forward and tapped PC Hydon on his arm. "It's an excellent idea. I love the drama! However, there's one small problem. We've no idea who did it!"

"Oh yes, we do!" said Frank.

Ella added, "We've been putting all the pieces of evidence onto our whiteboard."

Frank took over, "It's become like a logic puzzle that we used to set the children in school."

"We have all the clues there on the board. It's just a matter of putting them in the correct order. Then we'll have a solution." Ella crossed her arms and beamed with satisfaction.

WPC Knowle smiled, raised her hand as if to calm Ella down. "No, you won't have a solution. You'll have a theory. You'll need either hard evidence to back up your theory or a confession from the murderer."

"Either way, it's worth a go," Ella enthused, "At the very worst, the murderer will know that we're on his trail. He or she will be more likely to make a mistake."

"Or do a runner!" PC Hydon added.

"They won't dare, with you around." Frank teased.

"OK, here's another plan of action." WPC Knowle took command. "We'll do this when you've got a workable theory. Now, I'm off duty in about half an hour. So, if there's nothing else, I've got some paperwork to catch up on back at the station."

"I need to lock up this place and leave it all neat and tidy."

They all replaced their chairs under the table and went outside into the courtyard. Another immense effort, particularly from PC Hydon, and the Cider Vat was back where they'd first found it.

They went back through the kitchen, closed the back door and headed out the front.

"You said a plan of action?" Ella asked as they stood on the pavement in River Street.

"Are you on duty tomorrow evening? Frank added.

"No," both police officers replied together.

"Then you're invited to our house for a pleasant off duty meal. Roast beef with all the trimmings?"

"Certainly," the two replied. "Tell us where you live and we'll be there!"

"No problem," Ella said.

The next evening Ella and Frank prepared the proverbial roast beef with Yorkshire Pudding, roast potatoes and all the trimmings. WPC Knowle and PC Hydon turned up together out of uniform and dressed smartly casual. The atmosphere was relaxed and convivial. Frank broke out the bottles of Sowden Valley Select they'd bought in Cullompton. Ella suggested that to keep a clear head, it should be consumed in small and sporadic quantities only! Frank agreed.

Frank and Ella found out that PC Hydon was actually Alf Hydon in real life and WPC Knowle was known as Elsie when off-duty. Both police officers were happy for Frank and Ella to refer to them by their first names when they weren't in uniform.

"The uniform deserves respect!"

Ella and Frank had prepared the meal together during the day although Ella took over to serve up. Frank would inherit the washing up the next morning.

Alf consumed enough food to keep him from feeling hungry for at least a few days! Elsie ate less but was just as appreciative. At the end of the meal, when all was cleared away into the kitchen, everyone moved onto the sofa and armchairs in the front room. Frank leaned back in his chair, stretched his legs out over the white lambswool rug and put his hands together behind his head.

"We've spent all our spare moments today working on our whiteboard and we now think we know who killed Billy Bowd."

CHAPTER SEVENTEEN

THE THATCHED MEETING ROOM

It's not that I've been invited to the hole I'm standing in. It's that I accepted the invitation.

Elsie and Alf waited expectantly for an answer.

"I can't prove it without seeing the reactions of the suspects."

"So," shouted Ella, "we do need to go all Murder in Paradise!"

Elsie butted in. "Hold on, you can't just take over solving the crime. We're the police and it's our job to serve and protect you."

"Yes, I know," replied Frank, "but Ella's got a point. So far we've helped you quite a bit. If we can get the murderer to confess, then you'll still get the credit."

Alf rubbed his hands together and laughed. "This sounds fun. I'll stand guard at the door and if they try to escape, I'll stop them. They won't ever get past me!"

"True," said Ella.

"OK," said WPC Knowle, "I don't think my superiors would approve but I think I can see the benefit in this particular situation. If you can apply as much psychological pressure as possible when confronting the murderer with the truth then that could cause them to crack. You'll have a confession made in front of everybody."

"So?" asked Ella.

"OK, let's do it!"

Ella clapped her hands whilst Alf put up his hand.

"Yes, PC Hydon - Alf?"

"I like the idea. But before we get started, I'd just like to know one thing."

"What," said Ella.

"Who actually murdered Billy Bowd?"

"Isn't it obvious?"

"Well, no."

"Then you'll just have to wait and see."

Coffee and biscuits were served before the nitty-gritty of planning the meeting took place. Each suspect was to be invited.

"We can't use the police station. They wouldn't approve of us doing it Murder in Paradise style. It must be against all sorts of policies and procedures."

Ella had already thought about that. "Let's use the Thatched Meeting Room."

"You mean that lovely place halfway up Peak Hill Road?" Frank had seen the golden thatched circular building on one of their explorations around the Cotmaton area of Sidmouth.

"Good idea. I've heard from around the town that no one ever uses it these days," said Elsie.

"I'll book it for next Wednesday afternoon," said Ella.

Elsie and Alf consulted their phone diaries. "We can both be there, no problem."

Elsie volunteered to invite all the suspects. "The guilty ones will have to attend. If they don't attend, they'll be signalling their guilt to the rest of us. The innocent ones will want to come along to see who exactly was the murderer!"

Ella went into organisational overdrive. "Right, we set up the chairs in the middle of the room in a circle. The suspects can be all be seated there. We'll stand around the outside. Alf by the door, Elsie by the window."

"Ella and I will take turns to put forward all the motives, opportunities and alibis."

Elsie added, "We all need to watch the faces and body language of our suspects."

"Something will give the murderer away," said Frank with confidence.

"You arrest them," said Ella nodding at Alf, "Take them to jail. Do not pass go and do not collect £200." Ella was enjoying herself now.

Alf concluded the evening as he summed in apparent earnest, "Easy really. What can possibly go wrong?"

WPC Knowle spent the following day contacting Harry, Agnes, Gabriel and the Zummerzet Zyder Mafia. Unfortunately, Amelia was still in hospital and unlikely to be released in the next week or two. Agnes confirmed that she had a series of complex mental health issues that needed slow and steady treatment.

After a long phone discussion between the four of them, it was decided to continue with the meeting. Frank felt that if the meeting did not draw out the murderer, then it might, at least, point a finger at any of the suspects, including Amelia.

"Be there at two o'clock on the dot!" WPC Knowle told each of them, "Non-attendance could be considered a sign of guilt!"

All the suspects grudgingly agreed to the meeting. The mafia contingent declared it a complete waste of time. They were due to be blitzing the drinking establishments of Tiverton that afternoon not knowing that Harry may have beaten them to it. WPC Knowle reminded them again that if they didn't turn up then they may face a more formal and more thorough interview with the Exeter CID.

Ella booked the Meeting House. Frank and Ella went to visit the room before the meeting. There was one main door, a fire exit and a bay window with glorious views over Sidmouth and the sea.

"We'll put Alf by the door and Elsie by the fire exit. We'll stand in the bay window when we're not in the middle of the circle."

They found several comfortable chairs dotted around the room and formed them into a circle making sure the central area was big enough in which to comfortably walk around.

Ella then strolled around the room patting the chairs and straightening the curtains at the window. She moved one or two chairs imperceptible distances until she was completely satisfied. "That looks all OK to me!" she said.

"Good. Now we need to go over all the facts once more time. I want to check that we've got it all correct." Frank was feeling a bit nervous even though the meeting was not until next Wednesday.

"It's going to be all right, Frank," Ella stroked his arm and cuddled up to him.

"I hope so. I've watched it so many times on television. I've read all the Poirot novels over the years but this, this is the real thing. If we've got it wrong, then we'll have sent an innocent person to jail."

"No, we won't. We've been through it so many times. There is only one solution that makes any sense."

"Yes, you're right. It's just nerves - pre-match nerves or stage-fright."

"As Alf said the other day, what could go wrong?"

"True, but he also said that no-one ever gets murdered in Sidmouth!"

At one o'clock on Wednesday afternoon, Frank and Ella were in the Thatched Meeting Room once more setting the place up to their liking. By quarter past one, they were each sat down in one of the chairs checking their watches and showing visible signs of nervousness.

The clock on the wall above the door slowly moved around to half-past one. Apart from Frank and Ella, the place was empty. It was so quiet they could both hear the squawking of seagulls and the lapping of the waves on the beach down the road at Jacob's Ladder.

At a quarter to two, Alf arrived on foot. "WPC Knowle will along in 10 minutes. She's just issuing a reprimand to some people who dared to drop litter within her vicinity."

At one minute to two, WPC Knowle arrived in her police car. She parked it a little way down the road so, as she said later, "not to frighten any of the suspects any more than was necessary." She strode purposefully into the Thatched Meeting Room.

"Sorry, I'm late, everybody. Just executing my function as a police officer. Now I'm here, I'm going to have to transform myself into a passive observer."

"Not too passive. I hope we'll need you to make an arrest!"

She smiled and then stopped to look around. "Nobody here yet?"

"No, just the three of us - well, four now, with you!" Ella flapped her notebook on the side of the chair and looked worried. "What if no-one at all turns up?"

"Then Exeter CID will want to interview each one of them."

"CID scare me. Imagine what they'll do to our suspects." Alf's comments were cut off by the arrival of a Kia Sorento outside.

At five past two, according to the clock above the door, Delbert, Norbert and Albert marched rather unwillingly into the Meeting Room. They stopped just inside the door and looked around them. "Huh, to think we gave up Tiverton for this. It had better be worth our while!"

"I'm hoping that justice will be seen to be done. That's worth anyone's precious time." WPC Knowle smiled as she ushered them to three chairs in the circle.

"Are we being accused of this murder? Are we the only ones invited here this afternoon?"

"Be quiet and wait," PC Hydon said to them. They settled down silently taking in their surroundings. Even Delbert had run out of conversational quips. No death jokes from him today!

The clock ticked on to quarter past two.

Agnes Boyd was next to arrive followed closely by Harry Sowden. She was slightly out of breath having walked from the middle of Sidmouth past Jacob's Ladder and up Peak Hill Road. Harry arrived on his road legal quad bike complete with a trailer. It was not as muddy as they had seen it before. Someone had made an effort to tidy it up.

Frank and Ella stayed out of the way. They stood in the bay window alcove. It appeared they were in earnest whispered conversation. They were attempting to surreptitiously watch each of the persons in the circle for any telltale signs.

There were another three minutes of silence as the clock above the door moved onto twenty-five past two. Still, not everyone was here.

At half-past two, Gabriel arrived. "Sorry, I'm late. My bar staff didn't turn up on time. She's not the best of timekeepers."

"Neither are you," snapped PC Hydon. "Sit down on that chair over there!"

Gabriel meekly obeyed. Everyone in the circle gazed at WPC Knowle.

"Good afternoon, everybody. You are, of course, free to leave at any time. However, your actions may cause us to jump to conclusions that may not be of benefit to you!"

PC Hydon stood in front of the door, his head almost touching the lintel.

"I am here in an official capacity to maintain law and order. However, I am also here as an observer. Mr. and Mrs. Raleigh would like to take you through some thoughts they have had about the death of Billy Bowd."

Agnes sniffed. All eyes turned towards Frank and Ella as they moved into the middle of the circle of chairs.

CHAPTER EIGHTEEN

SO EVERYONE HAD BOTH MOTIVE AND OPPORTUNITY

The future, the present and the past walked into a bar. Things got a little tense.

Frank just about managed to smile as his gaze moved around the circle. He'd never felt so nervous. "Good afternoon everyone. Thank you for attending our little meeting. You were all acquainted with Billy Bowd. We thought you would all be interested to know how he died."

Ella took over. She was already starting to enjoy her performance.

"In collaboration with WPC Knowle and PC Hydon, we identified all those who had an interest in Billy's death. We have discovered how each may gain from his death. We investigated if any of our suspects had motives to kill him. We identified and checked each individual alibi."

"Wait a minute," said Gabriel. "Are you saying 'e was murdered?"

Ella nodded.

"And one of us may be the murderer?" added Harry.

Ella nodded once more.

"And we're your only suspects?" continued Delbert.

Ella nodded again.

"In that case, one of the people in this room is the murderer of Billy Bowd, my husband?"

"Yes, yes, yes and yes!" For the last time, Ella once more dramatically nodded.

"Well, this I must hear, "said Agnes once more.

"If I leave this meeting now?" interjected Albert making as if to stand and depart, "will that mean…?"

"You've already been warned of the consequences of your actions. If you make your way past me, then I'll arrest you on suspicion of the unlawful killing of Billy Bowd, sir," said PC Hydon. He stood minaciously by the door, completely filling the space.

Albert resumed his seat.

Frank stood in the middle of the circle and consulted his notepad.

"First of all, we asked ourselves, how would each of you gain from his death?"

Ella continued. "Let's start with the ladies. Amelia, if she were with us this afternoon would gain either from being able to live in Billy's house or to enjoy the proceeds of its sale. I think that she's a long way away from enjoying anything to do with life at the moment."

"Here, here!" agreed Agnes.

"And you, Agnes. Well, if you're not arrested for murder, then you'll be in receipt of a hefty payout from the life insurance. Thank your lucky stars that he kept up the payments every month without fail."

Agnes started to say "Only cos I…" but then she stopped and stared blankly out of the window instead. Ella took a step back and Frank assumed centre stage.

"The police agree with me that we have three more suspects. How would they gain from his death?"

WPC Knowle was watching with approving interest.

"Well, Gabriel, the landlord of the Mariner public house was conducting illicit cider smuggling. Billy brought the cider out of Sowden Valley Cider Farm and sold it to Gabriel. Gabriel admitted he'd had enough and was fed up with the whole business. Was he fed up enough to murder his next-door neighbour?"

Gabriel sat there looking down at the floor and shaking his head.

"And then there's Harry, the owner of Sowden Valley Cider Farm. He believed that Billy was stealing not only the cider but also the cider recipe. He believed he was going to sell to the high bidders not only the cider making secret recipe but also the inside story of the cider-making process."

All colour had drained from Harry's face. He looked defiantly back at Frank.

"Finally, we come to Albert Fitzhead, Norbert Fitzwarren and Delbert Fitzpaine, the self-proclaimed Zummerzet Zyder Mafia. What motive did they have to murder Billy Bowd?"

Albert put his sunglasses back on.

"Well, I'll tell you. They were out to get as much information as they could about Sowden Valley Select cider. The recipe, the process, what machinery was used. It was all useful. If they could buy out Sowden Valley, then they would have a foothold in Devon as well as Somerset. I think they were scared of Billy spilling the beans. Perhaps he was even blackmailing them as well."

Ella stood up and took Frank's place in the middle of the circle. "So that's the motives. Now, what about the opportunities?" She looked dramatically around the room.

"Every one of you had the opportunity to visit Billy that

fateful Friday."

Albert shook his head. "We were in Jersey. You know we were!"

"All three of you?"

"That's what I said."

"That's interesting because WPC Knowle did some digging around and found out that only two of you were in Jersey that day!"

"I was ill in bed with food poisoning all weekend," said Delbert quickly, a little too quickly.

"Convenient," Ella continued.

"Amelia and I were in Seaton," Agnes interrupted.

"True. But there was a gap of about forty-five minutes between you arriving back on the bus and then eating lunch at The Dairy Shop."

"But we were together."

"No, you told me that you split up and wandered through the shops in the High Street. Easily long enough to visit River Street. After all, we know Billy was killed at three minutes past twelve."

Agnes nodded. "Point taken!"

"Gabriel had plenty of opportunities to leave the Mariner pub and enter the house by either the front or back door. He knew all about the wooden gate behind the cider vat. He used it all the time."

Gabriel looked shocked as he realised the truth of Ella's accusation.

"That leaves Harry!"

"I told you I've not visited Sidmouth for over a year." Harry's face was still white and his voice still defiant.

"I think you have just told us a lie. A loud vehicle drowned out my conversation just as we got to Billy's house. In fact, it was a muddy, battered old quad bike with a trailer. It looks just like the muddy, battered road legal quad bike with a trailer that we saw at Sowden Valley Cider Farm. And just like the cleaned-up version that you drove here a short while ago."

"It could have been anybody."

"True, but we could always check with one of your workers. Gabriel's nephew for example. Metcombe. To see if you went out on your road legal quad bike with a trailer that day. I expect your diary will help us out as well, if necessary."

Harry's stare never wavered. "You're welcome to check. Anytime."

"You also visited Gabriel's pub for a business meeting, didn't you?"

Harry went silent and sullen.

"One more thing, Harry. Do you have a key to Billy's house?"

"Of course not. Why would I have a key to a house I've never visited?"

The sullen stare was still fixed on his face.

Frank stood up to take over. "So that's motive and opportunity. Unfortunately, it gets us no nearer the truth. Any one of you could have murdered Billy. Even Ella and myself."

Ella countered before she moved out of the circle. "However, our alibis have been checked by the police. It was impossible for us to have killed Billy."

"Unlike any of you!" Frank snapped.

Frank turned towards Harry.

"You told us you were in the Pannier Market in Barnstaple but then you told WPC Knowle you were in Tiverton. Make up your mind. Perhaps you were in neither Barnstaple nor Tiverton. Perhaps you were here on your quad bike in Sidmouth!"

Frank turned towards Agnes.

"You and Amelia had forty-five minutes in which to kill Billy. You know the hourly bus from Seaton arrives in Sidmouth at a quarter to the hour. You didn't get to the Dairy Shop until 12.30."

Frank wheeled towards Delbert.

"We only have your word that you were in bed with food poisoning. Perhaps the Land Rover or the Kia Sorento will turn up on the motorway cameras from that day? We'll need to check that, won't we?"

Delbert's facial expression almost shouted Go on, do your worst, I'm not scared! He looked calmly at Frank. "Please check your cameras. I've nothing to hide! And while you're at it, phone my dear mother, Doreen Fitzpaine. She lives in Norton Fitzpaine. Number seven, The Green. She may be eighty, but she hasn't lost her marbles yet. She'll confirm I was poisoned. She should know – she poisoned me!" Frank felt the desperation in his voice. Desperation to be believed or desperation that he might be found out?

PC Hydon quietly left his guard-post, opened the door and sidled outside. He took out his phone and dialled the police station.

Ella summed up. "So, everyone had both motive and opportunity. You all say you have an alibi – except each alibi is open to doubt."

Frank carried on. "Which brings us to the package."

"What package?" stuttered Harry.

Everyone in the room had an expression of surprise.

Frank smiled as Ella broke in. "We had a package misdelivered to our house on the day of Billy's murder. It should have gone to Billy. According to the Post Office, our addresses are similar. It's happened a few times before. They've muddled up our address and other houses on River Street. This time, we decided to take it around to his house ourselves. When we arrived, we put it behind the door on a small table. In all the commotion that subsequently occurred, we both forgot about it."

"It was only later that we remembered. However, when we went around to the house, with WPC Knowle, the package was no longer there. Neither was the key under the flowerpot."

"Flowerpot? Package? What are you talking about? Have we wasted a whole afternoon just because you lost a package and a key?" Norbert was baffled by this information.

"If you needed a key, you could have just borrowed mine," said Agnes.

"Or mine," added Gabriel.

"Or Amelia's," continued Agnes. "We all had one."

"Yes, we know that now," said Ella.

"You all had one except Harry and the Zummerzet Zyder Mafia."

The door opened and PC Hydon stuck his head back inside the room.

He whispered to WPC Knowle in a voice that easily carried throughout the room. "I thought you ought to know that Delbert was telling the truth about his food poisoning. I asked the station to phone Delbert's mum. She confirmed it and gave us the phone number of their doctor. I'm just going outside to phone him as well."

"Interesting," said Frank. "That leaves us with one person who knew about the package and where the key was hidden. It's now obvious to both Ella and myself that…"

Suddenly, without warning, Harry jumped out of his seat, knocked over Frank and crashed across the room and through the door. The startled group just watched. Ella and WPC Knowle moved into action and followed him but were halted by PC Hydon coming back in through the door. "He did have food poisoning. Hey, what's 'appening?"

"Please! Get out of the way," shouted Ella.

Both WPC Knowle and Ella made it outside. Over on the road was Harry's Quad Bike. Harry was jumping up and down attempting to start it. WPC Knowle raced down the road towards her car whilst Ella raced after Harry. As she got there, the machine burst into life. Harry threw it into gear and moved off up the road. Ella leapt at the rear trailer and managed to haul herself up on board.

CHAPTER NINETEEN

I'VE MURDERED ONCE. I'M ABOUT TO MURDER AGAIN.

It's not the fall that kills you; it's the sudden stop at the end.

Harry Sowden roared up Peak Hill Road, the steepness of the gradient didn't seem to affect the speed of the quad bike. He veered around the bend almost forcing Ella out onto the road. She grabbed hold of the edges of the trailer and repeatedly screamed at him "Stop! Stop! Stop!"

Harry took no notice. He didn't even acknowledge her existence. He appeared to be in some sort of trance staring straight ahead at the ever-changing horizon. At the top of Peak Hill, he swerved to avoid a car emerging from the car park on their right. He then executed a sharp turn through the open gates of the field that led to the Coast Path. He crashed, leapt and bounced his way over the uneven grassy field. Fortunately, there were no afternoon walkers in his way. Despite her predicament, Ella had time to realise that there would be no sheep to avoid because the gate was open.

A particularly violent bounce over a protruding grass mound refocused Ella's attention. Despite the bumpiness of the ride, Ella tried to move herself closer to Harry. She grabbed wildly at his back and starting thumping and punching with all her strength. She continued screaming at the back of his head. "Stop! Stop! Stop!"

Harry still took no notice. He must know I'm here, she thought. It appeared he did as the quad bike started veering from side to side deliberately looking for more of the many bumps and ridges in the field.

"Stop," she screamed, "You'll kill us both!" One part of Ella's brain tried to calmly take in her situation. The quad bike was going too fast for her to jump off the trailer. Anyhow, if she did, Harry would get away. She reached into her pocket for her phone. No signal. With blinding inspiration, she pressed record instead.

Harry continued to spur the quad bike across the field. To her horror, she slowly understood what he was probably aiming to do. He was heading at breakneck speed for the coast path and the cliff edge. He was going to drive through the hedge and over into the sea taking both himself and Ella to their certain deaths. This was no accident like Amelia's. This was the deliberate act of a murderer with nothing left to live for.

As the hedge came closer, Harry seemed to accelerate even faster. A group of walkers appeared if as from nowhere in front of them. Ella screamed; the group all screamed. Harry seemed startled back into conscious reality.

He swerved to avoid them, and the quad bike spluttered and skidded sideways into the hedge.

"Get away," screamed Ella, "he's gone mad! He's going to kill us all!" The walkers instinctively ran for their lives.

The hedge was well-built and sturdy. It had been reinforced with a stone base. The quad bike wheels left the ground and whirled helplessly in thin air as the body of the bike and its trailer came to a halt balanced precariously on top of the hedge. The engine died and Harry sat there stunned. Ella dare not look over into the watery void on her left. She slowly started inching her body closer to the right-hand side of the trailer to keep some form of equilibrium. She could feel the breeze rising from the sea below.

She spoke quietly to the driver, "Harry? What are you doing?"

He stared straight ahead, his whole head appeared to be white and sweating. In a tired, defeated voice he started talking. His words tumbled out in a torrent.

"It was me. I killed Billy. I didn't mean to. I went to his house to recover the package. He sent it to himself. Didn't want to smuggle it out, I guess. I got the package back later. You were there, weren't you? It contained all our processes - our unique recipe for Sowden Select. He was going to sell it all to the highest bidder."

Harry took a deep breath and continued. "It would have ruined me. I'm nearly bankrupt as it is. I would have lost the farm. All respect. My beautiful apples. I would have lost everything. I hit him with a vase. I didn't mean to kill him. I was just so, so annoyed with him."

He turned his head sideways towards the sea and spoke directly to Ella. She had never seen such a hollow, colourless, lost face.

"You worked it all out, didn't you? You got me. Well, that's it. It's over. I'm a murderer. I've ruined everything. It's all my fault. There's nothing worth living for."

Harry started crying with loud heart-wrenching sobs. The breeze rustled through the top of the hedge. The quad bike creaked unsteadily. Ella inched closer to the right-hand edge of the trailer.

Both Harry and Ella heard the police siren as WPC Knowle's car powered up Peak Hill Road, careered through the open gate and bumped at an excessive speed across the grassy field towards them.

"They're not going to take me to prison. I've murdered once. I'm about to murder again. Because I'm tipping this useless quad bike over the edge and we're going with it!"

Harry deliberately leaned over to his left towards the sea and Ella felt the quad-bike and trailer shift. She stood up and facing the opposite direction jumped for her life.

CHAPTER TWENTY

NEVER AGAIN

Solvitur ambulando 3

Retirement is wonderful, Frank thought. No more pressure and stress. No more looking at the clock. No more living by other people's expectations. No more... well, everything.

Frank and Ella were back strolling with Bella and George through the woods along the old railway track from the Bowd down towards Harpford.

"Makes you glad to be alive," declared Bella.

"Absolutely," said Ella.

"I'm so glad you jumped when you did. A few cuts and bruises are nothing compared with what could have happened."

Ella was starting to brim up with tears again, so Frank changed the subject.

"What glorious countryside. To think we're walking where trains once ran."

George was not so thoughtful. "It was brilliant of you to record all of his rantings before he...."

"George, be quiet," uttered Bella.

Frank never regretted for one nanosecond that they had become detectives for that short while. They solved the mystery. He did, however, deeply regret putting Ella in that life-threatening situation. "Never again!" he said out loud.

Ella was enjoying the walk and the companionship of their two friends. Retirement is wonderful. Except… you need something to live for. A reason to get up in the morning. You need an interest. The last six weeks had been some of the most exciting and fulfilling times of her life. The confession on the cliff hedge confirmed all of their theories. The police declared it Case Closed. Agnes and Gabriel went back to their lives in Sidmouth. Taunton Norton bought Harry's farm and plan to continue making Sowden Valley Select. Ella felt a sense of achievement in bringing a killer to justice. She also felt a sense of sadness in that Harry made a tragic choice that ended up costing him his life. Would she do it all again? She didn't want to say it out loud but never say never.

They crossed the East Devon Way and followed the old railway track down to Knapp's Lane, branched off to the right and ambled over the stone bridge and into Harpford village. They paused to admire the church of St Gregory the Great and the Edwardian Village Hall. They crossed the River Otter by the rickety metal bridge and trampled through the meadows back to the Recreation Ground car-park. They bid each other farewell and both couples headed for home.

As they parked their car in their driveway, Frank heard the phone ringing. He rushed indoors and picked it up just in time to hear the caller. "Thank heavens you're there, Elsie. Come quickly, I think Dudley's out to get me! He sent me a warning…"

"Hello," said Frank.

There was a pause.

"Ah, you're not Elsie? That's not 3511534, is it?"

The phone went dead.

POSTSCRIPT

Thank you for reading Cidered in Sidmouth. If you want to help spread the word about the book, then I'd appreciate it if you left a review on the Amazon book page. Please do it now!

If you want to receive up to date information about the East Devon Cosy Mysteries, please sign up for our newsletter. Newsletter subscribers will receive 6 walks in and around Sidmouth, an eBook that includes the walks Ella and Frank enjoyed in Cidered in Sidmouth.

To subscribe and to find out more about Frank and Ella Raleigh and their East Devon Cosy Mysteries please visit the author's website www.eastdevoncosymysteries.com

The author, PA Nash can be reached on:-

Facebook
www.facebook.com/pa.nash.182

Twitter
twitter.com/PANash49873070

Pinterest
www.pinterest.co.uk/EastDevonCosyMysteries/
or by
Email
info@eastdevoncosymysteries.com

A GOOD WALK

Solvitur Ambulando

A Latin phrase meaning "it is solved by walking." A good walk brings a new perspective on your problems and often allows you to solve them.

HARPFORD WOODS RAILWAY WALK

Newton Poppleford started as a Saxon 'new town' by the pebbly ford. The Roman Road from Exeter to the port at Axmouth crossed the River Otter not far from the present A3052 road bridge, which was built in 1840 by James Green, the first County Surveyor for Devon. It was one of only three bridges on the Otter to survive a great flood in 1968.

1. Leave the Recreation Ground car park in Newton Poppleford by turning left at the main entrance into Back lane. As the road bends left go through the gates and follow the footpath alongside the river for about 200 metres. Cross the footbridge over the River Otter and continue to the road.

You are now on the East Devon Way, a long-distance path from Exmouth to Lyme Regis that passes through both Newton Poppleford and Harpford. The Village Hall, on the right, before you reach the church, was built in 1902. It fell into disrepair and by the early 1980s was unusable and derelict with a leaking roof. Due to village volunteers, the Hall was completely renovated by 2004 with a new roof, floor and heating. In 2014 the Village Hall was bought from the Diocese and run by the villagers for the village.

2. Turn left at the road towards the church. At the church, turn left and then turn right up Knapp's Lane.

Harpford, previously known as Happerford, has a church described in 1878 by White's Devonshire as "a venerable fabric, consisting of nave, chancel, south; aisle, and a tower containing three bells. It has a wagon roof which has some curious carving." Harpford Church is dedicated to St. Gregory, but confusion with Harford in the Archdeaconry of Totnes has led to its being referred to sometimes as St. Nicholas. Augustus Toplady was Harpford's vicar from 1766 to 1768. The churchyard cross was restored in his memory with an inscription and quotation from his hymn 'Rock of Ages'.

3. As the Knapp's Lane road bends to the left, keep straight on and follow the East Devon Way footpath. Go through a kissing gate to enter Harpford Woods. Keep on this footpath ignoring any paths that branch to the left, including the East Devon Way as it branches to the left going under a tunnel. Keep the stream to your right and follow the path through the woods until you reach the road by the Bowd.

4. You may wish to stop for refreshments at The Bowd Pub. If not, then just before reaching the road turn a sharp left and follow the path of the old Sidmouth railway back through the woods.

The branch line from Feniton to Sidmouth was built by the Sidmouth Railway Company and opened in July 1874. Feniton station was immediately renamed Sidmouth Junction. The line from the Bowd to Tipton has 1 in 45 downhill run for 2 miles.

The first decades of the twentieth century saw the branch line at its most popular. In 1923 the Sidmouth Railway was absorbed into the Southern Railway. In the 1930s there was a peak of 24 services making the 30-minute journey each way between Sidmouth and Sidmouth Junction. The line eventually closed in 1967.

5. Just before crossing under a road bridge take the path to the right. This leads up to Knapp Lane, turn left and cross over the railway path following Knapp's Lane to Harpford Church. Retrace your steps back to the Recreation Ground car-park.

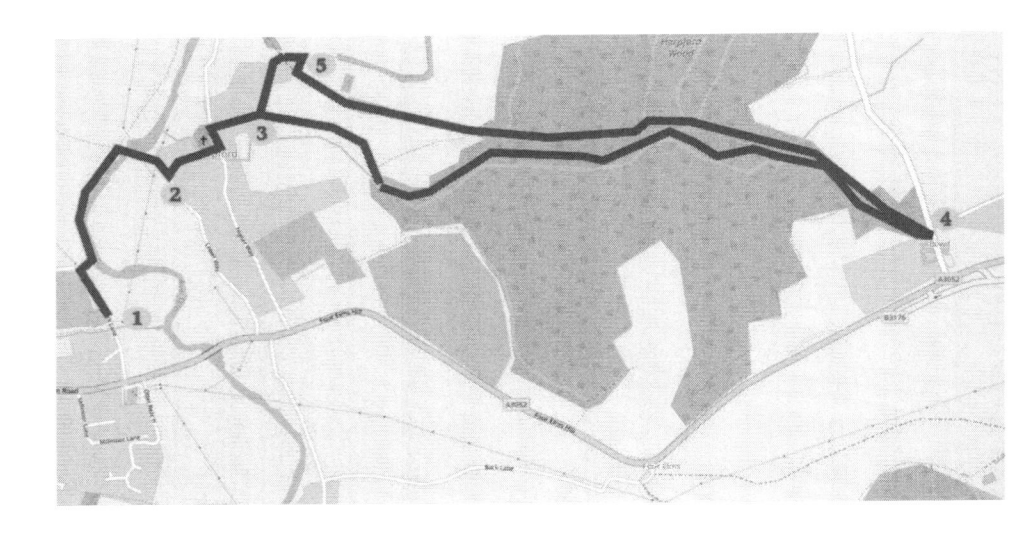

ABOUT THE AUTHOR

PA Nash and his supportive wife moved to glorious East Devon nearly a decade ago having taken early retirement from his previous job in South East England. Not quite ready for a life of endless relaxation, PA has since dabbled as a website administrator for the South West Coast Path, an IT office assistant in a local school and a WordPress website designer. This is his first cosy mystery book.

I've read so many cosy mystery novels in the past ten years. Some series like MC Beaton's Hamish Macbeth and Agatha Raisin were excellent, others not so!

I thought I could put together a series based around an area of England. Everyone's written about the Cotswolds and the Midsomer counties, so I thought it would be best to avoid those areas. We live in a beautiful part of the South West of England. East Devon is full of quaint villages, relaxing towns, peaceful countryside and hidden gems. It's just waiting for a few juicy murders! The police presence is minimal. The population is not as full of old-aged pensioners as some would have you believe. Perhaps it's time to create a rival to Midsomer!

I enjoy walking so I've made use of the South West Coast Path and other footpaths in my books. Each book will have a selection of walks most reasonably fit people can complete. Some of the walks can be found on the excellent South West Coast Path Association's website.

I intend to create a series of short cosy mysteries based around the towns and villages of East Devon.

THE DUDLEYS OF BUDLEIGH

"In the seventh hour of the night, on the seventh day of the year - you will die."

Anthony Buckerell received a note that simply delivered the fright of his complicated life.

"Dudley's out to get me!"

At 7.59, surrounded by police in a windowless locked cell, he did.

In the follow up to Cidered in Sidmouth, the genteel seaside resort of Budleigh Salterton is rocked by an impossible murder. Frank and Ella Raleigh find themselves reluctantly continuing as their delightful detective duo as delves into the lives of their suspects – each one named Dudley.

If you enjoy pacy whodunit cosy mysteries, then join Frank and Ella in the seaside resort of Budleigh Salterton getting to know some of the town's Dudleys as they head towards a traditional Golden Age denouement.

THE OTTERY LOTTERY

I'm giving away Kennaway Coopers, my company, to the winner of the Ottery Lottery!"

Caleb Kennaway's family and the other board members violently disagreed with his decision. A month later, Caleb Kennaway was found dead at the foot of the main stairs in Kennaway Court.

The third book in the East Devon Cosy Mystery series finds Frank and Ella Raleigh buying a ticket in the Ottery Lottery.

This leads them into an opportunity to investigate Caleb's death as well as a hunt for a miniature beer barrel that will change their lives.

CORN ON THE COBB

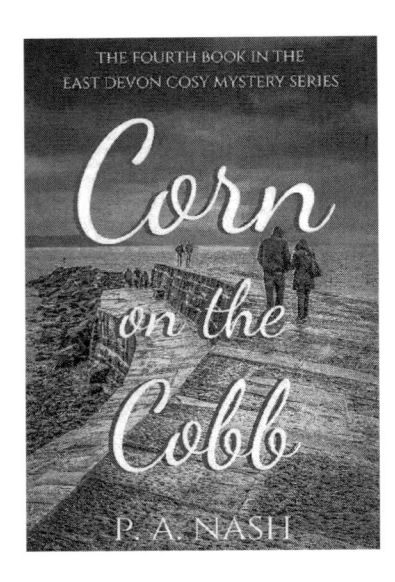

Pop backstage into the world of 60's chart star Cornelius Spooner for a mixture of music, murder and cosy mystery.

Meet Cornelius, his band, the Portobello Crooners and his six wives.

During a quiet weekend away at a Country House Hotel near Lyme Regis, Frank and Ella Raleigh find themselves caught up in their deadliest case yet.

Accidents? Murders? Suspects with alibis, motives and opportunities – it's all there.

Here's an excerpt from Chapter One of The Dudleys of Budleigh.

Parking the car on the gravel drive, Frank heard the phone ringing inside the house. He rushed indoors and picked it up just in time to hear the caller. "Thank heavens you're there, Elsie. Come quickly, I think Dudley's out to get me! He sent me a warning…"

"Hello," said Frank.

There was a pause.

"Ah, you're not Elsie? That's not 3511534, is it?"

The phone went dead.

"3511534…3511534…3511534," Frank repeated the number out loud whilst gesturing to Ella to find him a pencil or pen.

"I'm writing it down. You can relax. What was all that about?"

Frank sat down and explained to Ella. "A man said Dudley's out to get him. He thought he was phoning Elsie. He said that wasn't 3511534 and then put the phone down."

"I think you should try that number and see if it goes through to Elsie. Explain to her what happened. Whilst you're doing that, I'll put the kettle on!"

Ella went into the kitchen and Frank picked up the phone and dialled the number.

It rang for about ten seconds and Frank was about to cut off the call, when a female voice said, "3511534, hello, how can I help?"

"Hello," replied Frank. "Is that Elsie?"

"Yes, it is. I recognise that voice. It's Frank, isn't it?"

"How did you know?"

"You're speaking to a policewoman. We're trained to remember things."

"Elsie, WPC Knowle," Frank interrupted.

"Yes, that's me. How can I help? Is everything all right with Ella? She was such a brave lady."

"Yes, everything's great. I've just had a strange phone call. I think it was the wrong number. Someone said Dudley was out to get him and you had to come quickly."

"Ah, that'll be Arnold Buckerell. He's a solicitor over in Budleigh Salterton. He thinks someone is trying to kill him. He's a lonely old soul. A bit pompous and self-righteous. He needs a friend and he needs to get a life!"

Frank recognised the type. "A loner?"

"I guess he is, as far as his job will allow him to be."

"We used to have children like that at school. Always sat on their own in the corner of the playground. I used to have to work hard to bring them into a social circle that they could feel part of."

"Perhaps you could help here."

"How?" Frank felt he was digging himself into a hole and he wasn't sure how to clamber out.

"Come with me and see him. Offer him a sympathetic ear and use your schoolmasterly listening skills."

"Hmm," Frank hesitated.

"I'll go over there later this afternoon. If you want, I'll pick you up from Otterbury and we'll listen to his story and see if we can help."

Ella had come back into the room with a tray full of cups of tea and biscuits. She had heard the last part of Frank's part in the conversation. She nodded encouragingly.

"OK, it can't do any harm."

"Excellent, I'll see you at about half three."

Arnold worked in an office in the High Street above one of the flourishing gift shops that regularly spring up in seaside towns.

WPC Knowle parked right outside the office and she pushed open the door beside the shop-front. They both climbed the stairs before WPC Knowle knocked on another door that had faded gold lettering announcing that they were entering the offices of Anthony Buckerell LLB, LLP.

No-one answered her knock, so she turned the door handle and walked in.

A quiet, strained voice mumbled, "Come in."

"Too late, Anthony. We're already in!"

"Oh, it's you. Thank heavens!"

Anthony Buckerell sat, or rather slumped, in a wooden varnished but padded Bankers Chair behind a large mahogany Executive desk. The desk was clear except for a pristine blotter, an old-fashioned telephone and a couple of leather-bound A4 books. The wording appeared to read "Law Society" on the front cover.

"Dudley wants to kill me!"

"Good afternoon, Anthony, may we sit down?"

"Yes, pull up a chair. I see you've brought a detective with you. Good afternoon, sir, are you from Exeter?"

Frank sat down and smiled.

"Anthony, this is the gentleman you accidentally called earlier today. He's shadowing me and providing valuable feedback. You can rest assured that anything you say to either of us will be treated in a professional manner and in the strictest confidence.

"Good. I need all the help I can get!" Anthony was sweating and repeatedly ran his hand through his receding hair as if brushing it back out of his eyes.

WPC Knowle sat down and took out her black notebook. "Now, Anthony, how may we help you?"

Anthony looked up at Frank before his eyes travelled around to WPC Knowle. Then he looked down at his desk. "Dudley's out to get me. He sent me a letter. It said that I would…"

He buried his face in one hand. With the other hand, he pushed a piece of paper across the desk.

Frank picked it up and read aloud the printed words:

"You will die in the seventh hour of the night on the seventh day of the month."

Frank turned the piece of paper over. Nothing else. Just those seventeen words.

WPC Knowle took out her phone and checked the date. "It's the sixth of December today. That must mean tomorrow."

"I know! You needn't tell me what the date is. I know. Tomorrow. Tomorrow." His voice was becoming louder and more uncontrolled. "Tomorrow!" He shouted.

Printed in Great Britain
by Amazon